THE RANCH OF THE FOUR WINDS

THE RANCH OF THE FOUR WINDS
A WESTERN TRIO

WALT COBURN

SAGEBRUSH
Large Print Westerns

First published in Great Britain by ISIS Publishing Ltd.
First published in the United States by ISIS Publishing Ltd.

Published in Large Print 2014 by ISIS Publishing Ltd.,
7 Centremead, Osney Mead, Oxford OX2 0ES
by arrangement with
Golden West Literary Agency

ISBN 978–0–7531–5360–4 (pb)

Printed and bound in Great Britain by
T. J. International Ltd., Padstow, Cornwall

CONTENTS

Sin and Solitude

This story first appeared in Street & Smith's *Western Story Magazine* in the issue dated May 26, 1923 under the byline Walter J. Coburn. Now for the first time it has been collected in book form.

CHAPTER
ONE

"Them hills yonder?" The man with the deeply tanned face and large sombrero raised his soft voice so that he might make himself heard above the noise of the train. "Folks around here call 'em the Funeral Mountains, though why they picked that name for 'em I'm dog-goned if I know, 'lessen it's because it's so quiet there. That pointed butte on the left is called Buzzard Roost, and it's shore well named. All the buzzards in the Southwest cluster there, I reckon. Reckon it must be the water as draws 'em. Fine a spring as you ever saw at the foot of the butte cabin, too. I holed up there one fall when the prospectin' fever hit me strong. But in a month huntin' gold, the only companion I had was the chatterin'est magpie a man ever listened to. Reckon ol' Noisy Pete . . . that was what I called him . . . is still hoppin' in an' out the cabin door, cussin' me out aplenty in magpie for runnin' off from him that-a-way."

"Nobody lives there?" asked a rather pasty-faced young man who up to this time had taken no part in the conversation of his fellow travelers.

Todd McCloud's keen gray eyes held a humorous twinkle as he answered: "Reckon not, pardner. Buzzard Roost lies sixty miles from Caliente, the closest town.

And there ain't even a goat ranch between the town and the mountains. No water, that's the trouble . . . *sabe?* Nary a drop after you leave Caliente till your burros fill their bellies at Buzzard Springs. Not even the desert rats, the prospectors, goes out there any more. They've decided Funeral Mountains hasn't even a low-grade streak of gold in 'em. I was there a year ago, and I don't reckon there's been a human there since."

"I might go out there," suggested the young man, "if you thought I could stand the trip. I've come West for my health. Lungs," he explained, tapping his chest.

McCloud nodded. "It 'u'd be a good place to get well, stranger, and if you took plenty of water, you could make it. You can get an outfit at Caliente easy enough. Any of them greasers will sell you some burros. Two is a plenty. Prod 'em right along, and you'll do it in two days."

"I . . . I believe I'll try it," declared the young man, flushing a bit. "Caliente is the next stop, isn't it?"

"Shore is, pardner. You'd better be packin' your duds. And remember me to Noisy Pete when you get there. He likes biscuits . . . or flapjacks, if they ain't too hot."

Thus it came about that half an hour later George Chadwick stood on the sunbaked platform of the Caliente station, his two suitcases beside him, slowly tearing up his ticket to San Francisco and watching the disappearing smoke of the westbound flier.

A smile of satisfaction flitted across his sallow face, as he blew a cloud of cigarette smoke skyward. "This beats the bright lights . . . for a while," he muttered.

"Too much danger of some bull picking me up in the city. That hick tipped me off to the right place for little Georgie to lay low till folks forget, and the trail gets cold. Me for Buzzard Roost and solitude. I'll grow a set of whiskers that would fool the slickest dick that ever followed a clue. And not a soul knows where I am."

Perhaps George Chadwick would not have felt quite so well pleased with himself could he have read the thoughts of Todd McCloud, who was at that minute gathering his luggage, preparatory to leaving the train at Buena Agua, the next station, where he held down the more or less strenuous job of deputy sheriff.

"Something queer about that *hombre* that got off at Caliente," mused McCloud, as the porter carefully brushed off his hat. "Says he's a lunger, but I been in the same car with him since he got on at Chicago, and I never heard him cough once. And I've seen too many gents with the bug to be fooled. Don't like his eyes, neither. Kinda shifty. And he acted like he was makin' a getaway. I'll kinda keep an eye on that gent."

CHAPTER
TWO

"Another week of this solitude and I'll be insane!" George Chadwick muttered, as he left his look-out place up on the side of Buzzard Roost and started for the cabin at the foot of the butte.

For two weeks he had spent his waking hours in a high point on the butte, scanning the stretch of desert that lay to the south, smoking innumerable cigarettes and watching. True, the man on the train had said no one ever came to Buzzard Roost, and the appearance of the deserted cabin bore out the truth of that statement. Still there was always that remote chance of a visitor, and George Chadwick could ill afford to take any chances.

A close observer would have easily noted that each day wrought a slight change in Chadwick. Every night found him a bit more nervous. Sounds that had passed unnoticed those first nights now caused him to stiffen with apprehension. There were times during the night when he would wake from his sleep with a sudden start, his body bathed in cold perspiration, his shaking hand clutching the butt of his automatic in a viselike grip. Then he would sit upright in his bunk, scarcely breathing, a strange fear clutching his insides until he felt weak and nauseated. Soft rustlings overhead in the darkness, like the flutter of wings, weird scraping and scratching noises, their sound magnified by the intense darkness of the old cabin. The morning would find him tired and nervous. He now jumped at the slightest sound.

Reared in the city, Chadwick had never heard of pack rats that inhabited old cabins, or of bats that slept by day and fluttered about in the dark. Otherwise he might have slept more soundly.

Daylight brought but little relief. There was always that task of watching. While he lingered at the cabin, he was forced to endure the eternal chattering of the magpie. Noisy Pete was doing his best to live up to his name, and the constant chattering of the bird had got on the fugitive's nerves. He wasted good ammunition trying to kill the pest, but he was too poor a marksman to accomplish stilling the voice of Noisy Pete. As the days went by, Chadwick grew to regard the bird with an unreasoning blind hatred. He thought he detected an accusing note in the magpie's constant chatter.

Perched on a mesquite limb, Noisy Pete would scold all during Chadwick's meal. Sometimes the scolding would take on an almost human sound. "Murderer! Thief!" Chadwick thus interpreted the chattering.

Mad with fury, the man would hurl missiles at the bird, but to no avail. Noisy Pete was persistence personified. And again there were those oddly shaped boulders on the side of the butte that towered above the cabin. Were they shaped like tombstones, or was that some devilish twist of his tortured brain? And there were the huge flocks of buzzards that perched on them, or soared about overhead, in an everlasting line to some dead thing in the desert beyond, returning at sunset to perch on the very threshold of his cabin. Were the things waiting for him to die? The bray of a burro would make him whirl, gun in hand, a look of hunted fear in his pale eyes, his face distorted and drawn.

Sometimes, as he sat on the hillside, Chadwick would take a chamois bag from his pocket, spread a handkerchief on the ground, and empty the contents of the bag on it. As the sunlight bathed the handful of diamonds, sapphires, and rubies, an insane light of joy would come into the man's eyes. Carefully he would take them in his hand, let the precious gems trickle through his fingers, muttering softly to himself in a gloating, crooning way. Reluctantly he would count them and store them away. The hunted look would come back into his eyes. For always the memory of the thing he had done to obtain those jewels would come to haunt him.

Again he would see the horror and fear that stamped the features of old Isaac Chadwick, his uncle, as he had beaten the old man into insensibility, then continued the beating until the old man's life had gone from his old body. "If only the old fool hadn't found his speech," Chadwick would mutter over and over. "And begged for his worthless old life. He'd been dumb all his life, or nearly all of it. Paralyzed, all except his eyes that blazed like two bright-blue lights. What did an old paralytic like that want to live for, anyhow? Dumb as a post for all those years, then when he saw me get the jewels from under his pillow . . . that night, with the moon shining in through the window . . . the eyes blazed and words came from the mute. Harsh, uncanny, a dead body talking . . . begging for the jewels . . . threatening. How he had pleaded for his miserable old life, as the blows from the chair rained on his twitching white head. Only for that recovery of lost speech, I would have let the old fool live."

Chadwick had begun to discover something in the chatter of the magpie that sounded like the voice of old Isaac Chadwick, and the feel of that chamois bag in his breast pocket served as a constant reminder of the dead man. He stopped on his way down the hillside, emptied the jewels in the pocket of his coat, and threw the bag away. He felt a trifle better for a while. Then came the fear that some of the precious bits of stone might get lost. A good hiding place would be the thing. Even as the thought struck him, he remembered a hollow stump of a burned sycamore near the cabin. The very place. There was a hole in the side of the charred trunk, a foot in depth and some six inches in circumference.

He had discovered the hole by accident one morning, while examining the old tree that had years before been shattered and burned by lightning. He chuckled to himself, as the idea grew. He would be rid of actual contact with the plunder. It would no doubt aid his peace of mind. Then if he could rid himself of the magpie, he reasoned, his days at least would be easier to endure. He had made up his mind to spend a month at Buzzard Roost, then move on toward San Francisco, sell the jewels, and live a life of luxury. He was in an almost pleasant frame of mind when he reached the tree at the foot of the butte.

Carefully he cleared the hole of its debris of dirt and twigs, scraped the charred interior till it was smooth, and counted the jewels, one by one, as he dropped them into it. "Twenty," he said, "an even twenty. A tidy sum they'll bring in to me some fine day. No use to cover 'em. There isn't a soul to see 'em, and I hate to get 'em all messed up by throwing dirt in on top of 'em. They're as safe there as they'd be in a vault."

He even managed to whistle a bit of jazz, as he prepared his evening meal.

Morning found him a bit haggard. Twice he had wakened during the night. Perhaps it was the subconscious thought that the chamois bag and its precious contents were not under his pillow as usual, or, perhaps, it was his dream of Isaac Chadwick's accusing eyes that caused him to toss and mutter in his sleep, then awake with a start to lie for hours trembling with nameless fear. At any rate he spent a bad night, and dawn found him dressed, with breakfast on its way.

His vigil that day was divided between the strip of desert that lay in the direction of Caliente and the stump where he had cached his loot. He could not see the tree itself, only the brush surrounding it. A man could, by carefully skirting the base of the butte, approach the cache unseen by the watcher.

Chadwick found himself growing uneasy. Perhaps he was not the only man that inhabited the Funeral Mountains. There might be other springs in the adjacent hills. Because he had seen no one was no sign there were no other men in the hills. Perhaps that man on the train had deliberately sent him to Buzzard Butte — had suspected him all along. It was not impossible. The more he thought of it the more his uneasiness increased. He could hardly wait for sundown to get back to his cache. He fell twice in his descent of the steep mountain side, so great was his haste.

His fingers were trembling, as he shoved his hand into the hollow tree. Beads of sweat stood on his brow, as he brought forth the jewels and counted them. A hoarse cry burst from his dry lips, as he finished the count. He shook like a man with ague, as he again thrust his hand in the hole. Trembling, faint with nausea, he sat on the ground and counted the jewels over and over. Always the count was the same. Twelve. Eight of the jewels were missing.

It was dark when Chadwick rose and crept toward the cabin. Stumbling, muttering to himself, he stealthily approached the shack. He half expected to see someone there. The jewels were in his left-hand coat pocket, tightly clutched in his hand. His right hand held his automatic. A sudden chattering from Noisy Pete, almost at his elbow, caused Chadwick to whirl and shoot at the sound, then curse insanely at the bird.

He examined the cabin minutely. Not a thing was disturbed. It was a night of terror for George Chadwick. He sat all night in a corner of his cabin, his gun in his hand, peering into the dark, straining his ears to catch the slightest sound.

Daylight brought a slight return of courage. He became calmer after he had forced himself to eat and had downed several cups of strong coffee. For the first time he began to reason the thing out. Why had only eight of the jewels been taken? To frighten him? Most likely. Whoever had taken them would return, of that Chadwick felt certain. As he ate, he decided on a plan of action.

He would replace the rest of the jewels in the tree, then lie in wait for the thief's return. No use to look for tracks; he was not schooled in the ways of the open places to detect a trail on the hard ground. The man would come through the brush, along the base of the butte. He would take a position from where he could command a view of the tree. He would have to go about this business carefully, if he was to succeed. He would leave the cabin, replace the jewels in the tree, and start on up the mountain. Then doubling back and taking care to hide his movements, he would take a position from where he could see his cache. He put an extra clip of shells for the automatic in his pocket and left the cabin.

A look of crafty desperation was in his pale-blue eyes as he dropped the precious stones in the hollow of the tree and started on his trail. Upward he climbed till he was out of sight of the cabin and tree, hidden by the brush and boulders. Then he began to circle back toward the cache. This took time, and there were times when he lost sight of the tree stump. It was almost an hour before he reached the hiding place he had selected. He wondered if, during those times when the cache was lost to sight, his enemy could have been there. That was hardly probable. It would be later in the day most likely before the man would pay another visit.

Noisy Pete, locating Chadwick, set up a great chattering. From a safe distance the bird scolded at length. Chadwick, raging, was almost tempted to try a shot at the bird. It was with difficulty that he suppressed the desire. After a time the magpie seemed to weary of his scolding tirade and flew elsewhere. Chadwick sighed with relief.

The sun mounted higher in the cloudless sky. It grew warm, and with the increasing heat Chadwick began to grow sleepy. His sleepless vigil of the previous night had left him worn out. From where he sat in the brush he could not see the circling buzzards, nor the tombstone-like boulders. Quiet enveloped him, then drowsiness, which he half-heartedly fought off. At last sleep conquered, and for hours Chadwick slept the deep sleep of utter exhaustion. Not even the frequent chattering of Noisy Pete could rouse him.

It was nearing sundown when Chadwick awoke with a start. He could scarcely believe his eyes, as he beheld the sun setting. Muttering to himself, he rose to his feet. "Slept like a fool. Serve me right if he's taken the rest of the diamonds. Oh, what an idiot I am!"

Fearfully he approached the cache and thrust his hand inside. A gasp of surprised anger preceded a cry of anguish, as he withdrew his hand — empty! Not one of the precious gems remained.

Sobbing brokenly, his features convulsed in a horrible, twisted distortion that was scarcely human, he

13

threw himself on the ground, screaming. Fear had left him, giving way to insane rage.

After a long time his sobbing ceased. Like some wild animal he rose from the ground. His hands were torn and bleeding, where he had clawed at the ground, and on his thin, twisted lips were flecks of dried, bloody foam. The man was insane.

George Chadwick did not return to the cabin that night or the next day. Babbling broken sentences that held no meaning, his clothes torn to rags, his flesh lacerated and grimy with dried blood, he crawled through the brush, hunting — hunting he knew not what.

Across the sixty miles of desert that lay between Caliente and Buzzard Roost, a horseman rode at a steady trot that ate up the miles with surprising rapidity. He carried water for himself and his mount. But, despite the fact that Todd McCloud was astride the best road horse money could buy, it was almost dark when he drew rein at Buzzard Springs.

He glanced about him, his keen eyes peering into the shadows of the brush. Without delay he unsaddled and hobbled his horse, then walked boldly toward the cabin. McCloud knew he was taking a chance in thus boldly searching for the man he wanted, the man whose picture was on the placard underneath the printed notice of a $1,000 reward for the capture, dead or alive, of George Chadwick, murderer. But McCloud was of the breed that scarcely knows the meaning of fear.

14

Moreover, he had a certain contempt for Chadwick and his sort.

With his .45 held ready for opening any argument, McCloud kicked open the cabin door. For a minute he stood peering into the dark, then with a snort of contempt for the prowess of the man he sought, he struck a match.

The cabin was empty. McCloud lit a candle that stood on the rude table. By its flickering light he examined the cabin.

"*Hmm*," he mused. "Something sorter queer about this lay. Dishes dirty . . . grub in the skillet that's as stale as if it was there a week. Coffee in the pot gone sour. Nobody bin in this shack for several days. I'd think the varmint had pulled out, only I saw his burros at the spring, and his stuff is all here. Shore looks queer to me. Well, can't do a thing tonight. Reckon I'll clean the dishes and take on a little chuck. And that bed yonder looks plumb invitin'."

Todd McCloud slept soundly despite the fact that he was in the very bed of the man whom he sought. Ever a heavy sleeper, he did not awake when a stealthy step sounded in the cabin. Not until the intruder struck a match and lit the candle did his eyes open,. He did not move, but lay rigid, his fingers wrapped about the butt of his gun. It took a man of iron nerves to lie quietly in the presence of such a creature as stood revealed in the dim light of the candle.

Ragged, bloody, his straw-colored beard and hair matted and clotted with filth, George Chadwick crouched beside the table. His eyes glittered with the

15

fire of insanity, and he looked wildly about the room. Finally he saw the face that showed above the blankets of his bunk. His thin lips bared in a hideous grin, as he edged toward the man who lay motionlessly in bed.

"I knew you were here, curse you!" snarled Chadwick. "Been here every night, haven't you? I couldn't see you before, but I heard you, didn't I? Heard you and was afraid of you. But I'm not afraid of you now. I'll send you back to where you belong, only I'll make you fork over the diamonds before you go! Came back and got 'em, eh? Came back to get the pretty rocks you loved better than you love your flesh and blood."

Chadwick was edging closer as he spoke, his eyes never leaving the deputy's face. Then he sprang like a wild beast, straight at McCloud's throat. Starved and wasted as he was, the man seemed to possess the strength of ten men. The deputy struggled in vain to free himself from those terrible hands that were choking his breath from him. His six-shooter had caught in the blanket when he tried to wing the man who attacked him. Chadwick had torn it from him with the same ease that a man takes a toy from a child. Gasping for breath, the blood pounding his temples like a trip hammer, McCloud fought without avail against the talon grip of this madman. His senses reeled, and he grew limp and helpless. Then Chadwick's grip slackened, and, as if in a dream, McCloud heard the insane man asking over and over: "Where are they? Where are the jewels? Where have you hidden them this time, you old . . . ?"

With great gasps, that stabbed like a knife, the deputy gulped lungs full of air. His strength came back, and he found himself gazing into the insane eyes of the man who bent over him. Chadwick kept questioning McCloud, and the madman's long fingers were still about his throat, loosely held.

Summoning all his strength, McCloud's arms shot up and around Chadwick's trunk. With a quick twist the deputy threw the struggling man to the floor, and they rolled over and over, locked in desperate embrace. Suddenly Chadwick went limp, his head sagged, and he fainted. Nature had conquered. Matter had conquered over mind. The insane will that had lent superhuman strength to the weak body had given way, and George Chadwick was as helpless as a child.

"Whew!" gasped McCloud, as he bound the feet of his prisoner and gingerly felt of his bruised throat. "Reckon I shore learned a lesson from that session. These loco gents is shore tough *hombres* in a rasslin' match. From now on I shoots 'em first and talks to 'em after, takin' chances of their bein' able to answer. I wouldn't have missed that show for a spotted pony, but I ain't cravin' none for no encores. No, ma'am. I like to got on speakin' terms with the angels that last two hours he had aholt of me."

CHAPTER
THREE

The next morning, as Todd McCloud sat in the shade of the cabin, he smoked reflectively, trying to piece together bits of Chadwick's rambling talk. He was sure that there was something about the man's raving that hinted of a chapter in this strange drama of which he was unaware. The information he had gleaned regarding the crime and its motive laid stress on a valuable collection of precious stones that had been the property of the murdered man. It was supposed that these jewels were the motive for the brutal killing. Chadwick must have hidden them somewhere, but an exhaustive search had given no clue other than the trampled brush and grass around the charred stump of the old hackberry tree.

A noisy chattering broke in on the deputy's reverie. He looked up with a grin. "Howdy, Pete! Dog-goned, if I hadn't clean fergot you, pardner. How's tricks? Did the loco pilgrim feed you? You cuss me out like you'd bin plumb abused."

The magpie, with the boldness that is characteristic of his species, hopped closer, inspecting his old friend with ludicrous sagacity. Here was a man who spoke kindly, a man who might prove a friend. Warily he

18

inspected his old playmate, cloaking the inspection with a continuous petulant scolding.

McCloud, hugely pleased, brought some scraps of biscuit from the cabin and fed the magpie that hopped about, picking up crumbs. His hunger satisfied, he perched on a rock nearby and chattered.

"Wonder if you still have your old tricks, Pete?" questioned the deputy. He fished about in his pocket till he found a dime that was of recent coinage and quite bright. He tossed it out on the ground, not far from Pete. In an instant the magpie had it in his bill and was gone. McCloud followed leisurely. "Ought to have quite a collection in that cache of yours by now," he said, walking toward an old box into which the magpie had disappeared.

Ten minutes later Todd McCloud retraced his way to the cabin, followed by the scolding magpie. The deputy was grinning widely, and in his hand was the dazzling little collection of gems for which one man had lost his life and another man his sanity.

"You danged ol' thief!" McCloud chided the scolding bird. "Cached the loot in the stump yonder, and you found 'em, eh? No wonder the poor devil was spooky."

"A fool for pets," they call Todd McCloud in the town of Buena Agua, and it surprised no one when he brought home a magpie from Buzzard Roost — brought him along in a rudely constructed cage tied to his saddle horn, despite the fact that he walked most of the way, his horse being ridden by a crazy man lashed into the saddle.

19

"He's a kind of a sub-deputy, gents," McCloud explained. "And a shore good one. But keep yore eye on yore jewelry while the little cuss is around. He plays the law from both ends, and he can shore cuss in bird talk when you pinch him. Eh, Pete?"

The Gun Highway

This story first appeared in *Action Stories* under the byline Walt Coburn in the issue dated August, 1928. It was subsequently reprinted as "Renegade Rancho" in *Action Stories* in the issue dated June, 1937. Its original title has been restored for its first appearance in book form.

CHAPTER
ONE

From a certain little bay on the eastern shore of the Gulf of California to the well-kept Old Trails Highway that runs from California across Arizona, the airline distance is approximately sixty miles. There is a fact to conjure with if you are at all interested in the unlawful but highly profitable business of smuggling. No signpost marks that uncharted route from the little anchorage across the international border between Mexico and the United States. But among certain men it has a name. They call it *El Camino de Chinos* that, put into English, means the Highway of Chinamen.

Years ago, when the smuggling of Chinamen was in its early stages of development, a red-faced, walrus-whiskered saloon man known as Bismark made a snug fortune handling smuggled Orientals. He would meet a boat at the little bay. The skipper of the boat would pay into the calloused hand of Bismark $500 a head for the Chinamen landed. Whereupon Bismark would count the money, grunt his thanks, and herd his aliens northward. He rode a tough roan mule. The Chinamen walked.

In the rainy season this sixty-mile trek was not so bad. But during the dry months that journey across the cactus-strewn wasteland was tortuous, for the nearest water hole was ten miles north of the border and fifty miles from the little anchorage from where they started. Because Bismark had neither the time nor inclination to bury those who perished along that terrible trail, its course could be followed by the bleached skeletons of those unfortunate Chinamen who died en route.

In later years, when smuggler rules decreed that the price per head be paid on delivery upon American soil, Bismark renounced the business of smuggling. He was content to tend bar. He had made his fortune anyhow. Visitors at the border town where he did a thriving business spoke of Bismark's bluff cordiality. They spoke of him as being a genial old Dutchman. And the devil and Bismark alone knew the black tally of dead men against his record when he died a year or two ago. For many of those bleached skulls bore a round hole between the eye sockets.

Ask some leather-faced, keen-eyed man of the Border Patrol what he knows of El Camino de Chinos. Watch his jaw muscles grow taut and his eyes narrow a little. If he is of profane nature he will swear softly but with fervor. For it would take a small army of riders to patrol properly that strip of desert borderland from Yuma to Nogales.

Two of the Immigration men now pulled off the main highway in a striped car. They munched in silence on some stale sandwiches and washed down their food with warm water carried in a flannel-covered canteen. Their uniforms were dusty and needed pressing. Their eyes were red from loss of sleep. There was a grim look to the set of their jaws as they took up their post.

The hum of a high-powered motor heralded the approach of a car. The younger of the two officers took a sign from the dusty car. This sign was fastened on an iron framework and when placed in the center of the highway read: **Stop. U.S. Immigration Officers**.

A seven-passenger car of expensive make, its khaki top and shiny black body powdered with yellow dust, slowed to a smooth halt. The driver, a huge man wearing an oversize Stetson hat, grinned and nodded. The four passengers in the rear seats exchanged glances of mild inquiry.

"Howdy, boys!" The driver was tanned, handsome in a heavy-jawed, florid way. His smile displayed a set of surprisingly white and even teeth. But the gray eyes under the wide hat brim were cold and unsmiling. On the door of the car and on the tailored tire cover was neatly printed: **Seven-Up Ranch.**

"Hello, Mister Liggett," said the younger Immigration officer, grinning. He did not even glance inside the car but kept eating his bacon sandwich.

"How's tricks, Sam?" boomed the man in the big hat who was known from San Diego to El Paso as Jack Liggett, owner of the biggest dude ranch in the Southwest.

"Same old seven and six," replied the overworked Immigration man. "Bouncing here and there like a Mex jumping bean."

Sam's partner strolled up, smiling a weary greeting.

"I talked my head off when I was on the coast, trying to get more men along this patrol." Liggett passed out a handful of foil-wrapped cigars. "But I don't suppose it'll come to anything. I'm paying five men good wages to ride the strip of border along my place. I told 'em so, too. Well, boys, drop in any time at the *hacienda*. Glad to have you. So long!"

Liggett let in the gear and the motor purred. The passengers eyed the men in uniform with no little curiosity. The car swung along the graveled road, hidden in a cloud of dust.

"The lucky stiff," grunted Sam, dividing the cigars. "Soft graft he has with his dude ranch. Four more guests that'll be payin' him plenty money to ride a horse around over the mesas. He works 'em, too. Has the fools helpin' him round up his cattle. Gee, boy, did you see the peach in the back seat? Some girl. And Jack'll tax her twenty bucks a day to stay at the Seven-Up. Mama!"

"You didn't look in his car, Sam?"

"Look in Liggett's car? What for? That guy has plenty *dinero* without smuggling chinks. Fifty thousand acres well stocked with white-face cattle, a dude ranch that pays him big. When you've been on this strip of the border a while, you'll savvy Jack Liggett. He's a good guy. Always stops to chew the rag. Never forgets to pass out cigars or cold beer or some grub. Now and then when I get near his place, I drop in. Jack treats a man like he was a payin' guest."

The other man nodded. He was older than Sam, new to that section of the patrol. But he had put in two years at Tijuana and Mexicali and it took more than a grin and couple of good cigars to get behind his guard. He had seen a flicker of danger in the cold gray eyes under the $60 Stetson. But he said no more about Jack Liggett. The owner of the dude ranch had sold himself to Sam for the real article. When a young man of Sam's caliber is opinionated, argument is useless.

"Sam," he asked casually, "where does this *El Camino de Chinos* lay?"

"South, Tex. See those dim peaks yonder? Well, it runs to the east of them. Those are the Gila Mountains. The old Chinaman trail crossed the Lechuguilla Desert east of the mountains. There's a short creek runs there. In dry seasons it's just a string of water holes. A strip of hell, I'll tell the world. There's some old volcanoes down there. There's a spot where a man can stand and look down into the old craters of three extinct volcanoes. Down on the floor of those holes are big ironwood trees. From the rim, they look like greasewood bushes. Lots of mountain sheep in there. But there's a bunch of *muy malo* Injuns that hang out in that country. Not many white men ever been across there. Old Bismark, they claim, knew the country and stood in with the natives. That may be all a lie like most of these desert yarns. I know I wouldn't go down *El Camino de Chinos* for five years' pay."

Tex Lowry had a worried look in his eyes and his mouth was a grim line. "This is the dry season, ain't it?"

"Ain't had a rain in months." Sam nodded.

"It'd take a good horse to come up *El Camino de Chinos*, I reckon," Tex mused aloud.

"A good horse, Tex, and a hell of a good man."

"Yes," agreed Tex Lowry, "a hell of a good man."

CHAPTER
TWO

Skeleton Bay is the name that the smugglers gave the little anchorage on the east coast of the Gulf of California for its shore is strewn with the whitened bones of many whale carcasses. The Indians claim that the whales came into the bay to die and the tides washed the dead bodies up on the shore. It may be that whalers towed their harpooned kill into this quiet water and there on the sandy shore stripped their blubber. At any rate the bones are there, vertebrae wide as the span of a tall man's arms, huge ribs ten feet long, scoured white by water and sun and wind.

A sapphire sea slaps its foamy breakers against a sand-duned shore. The deathly silence is broken only by its tides and the screams of gulls. The sun blazes down from a cloudless sky. Despite the beauty of the place it is not a spot where a man would wish to linger. One is reminded of galleons anchored out there, of a blindfolded man walking the plank, of blood-soaked bandages and pieces of eight, of buried treasure and its dead men standing eternal watch. It is an ill-omened spot shunned by the natives.

The man who sat a sweat-streaked horse in the bright sunlight of the morning had no fear of ghostly things. His puckered blue eyes took in the splendor of the sea that glistened in the sunlight, the flight of the gulls against the sky, the white sand. He smiled a little with sun-cracked lips, but there was a grimness to that smile that robbed it of any humor.

"I reckon, Biscuits," he spoke to his buckskin horse, "that we've done found 'er. This is the place. Purty, eh? Purty, like a laid-out corpse."

He was deeply tanned; a stubble of sand-colored whiskers stood out like bristles on his square jaw. A short, straight nose and the blue of his eyes hinted of Irish ancestry. His hair was reddish brown, a little sun-streaked as if he were in the habit of going about without a hat. His clothes were those of a working cowboy — overalls, jumper, cotton shirt, and bull-hide chaps scratched colorless by brush. A high-crowned Stetson shaded his eyes. A well-filled cartridge belt sagged about his waist supporting a Colt .45. He rode along the shore, leaning down from the saddle as his eyes swept the sand for tracks.

"Here we are, Biscuits." He pulled up and dismounted. For almost five minutes he stood there, reading the sign of footprints in the sand. "Made yesterday," he thought aloud, "at low tide. That'd be along toward evening, according to the tide chart. A skiff landed three men. Then the skiff must 'a' pulled out and left 'em. They stood around a while, then started out afoot, toward yonder dunes."

Leading his horse, he followed their trail into the dunes that were carpeted sparsely with a growth of salt grass. In a little hollow between the dunes he came upon the ashes of a fire, some empty cans that had provided a meal of tomatoes and canned meat for someone who had camped there for about the fire the tracks of a fourth man predominated. This man wore high-heeled boots, whereas the other three tracks were of men whose feet were covered in broad-heeled, wide-soled shoes.

The blue-eyed man nodded his satisfaction. "A feller waited here and met them three. He's the guide. And right here is where he led up three mules and mounted the three gents. He's on a horse. Mules and horse all shod. They pulled out about the cool of the evening. Headed north."

He mounted his horse and followed the trail made yesterday. For a mile or more, he followed the trail, then swung off at a tangent, the buckskin horse hitting an eager trot. Half an hour later he came upon a laden pack mule that stood tied to a mesquite. The mule greeted his coming with loud braying. The horse nickered reply. The man swore at them in a good-natured drawl. "Well, now, ain't it just too bad that you two got separated for an hour! Now you're cussing me out for a sure mean specimen, eh? And incidentally you two boneheads are making enough racket to be heard back at Yuma. Sounding off like two buglers calling assembly. Want to get a good man shot? I'd swap you both off for a couple of magpies."

He untied the mule and tucked its hackamore rope up under the rope that held the pack. "From here on, Dynamite," he told the mouse-colored mule, "you keep that mezzo-soprano voice of yours salted down in brine, or I'll put a dash of strychnine in your grain. Come on, babies, we're following some skunks."

He swung back to the tracks and followed them along. He had gone perhaps five miles and the dunes had hardened out into a level country covered with greasewood and a forest of giant Saguaro cactus. Ahead were blue peaks, distorted in the heat waves.

Biscuits snorted and halted. Dynamite's long ears were two furry question marks. The man's gun was in his hand in a split second as he peered ahead along the trail. Not a hundred feet ahead lay the motionless body of a man. Two buzzards lifted their black wings and took flight. The man on the buckskin horse sheathed his gun. Buzzards do not perch on anything but the dead.

He dismounted and kneeled beside the dead man. It was the body of a young man in his twenties, dressed in cotton shirt, khaki riding breeches, and cavalry boots. The gun scabbard under his armpit was empty. There was a bullet hole between his shoulders. His hat was gone and his fair hair, thick and inclined to curl, was flecked with sand as if he had fallen from his horse, dead even as he hit the ground — shot through the heart from behind. He had not been dead many hours. The two buzzards had just found the body.

"You won't hold it against me, old man," spoke the blue-eyed cowboy, "if I go through your pockets."

But the search revealed nothing. No shred of identification was left. They had even taken his gun.

"A boy," said the man with the puckered blue eyes, "who was just beginning to live. They got you from behind, buddy. And they'd have left you like this. Ah!" He leaned across the dead boy, and as gently as he could he slipped a seal ring from the dead hand. It was a gold ring with a monogram engraved upon its seal. The monogram was filled with black enamel. **R.L.** were the initials. "Whoever you are, buddy, we'll give you the best we can in the way of a burial. We'll keep the ring those skunks overlooked. If the *Señor Dios* is kind, we'll mebbyso someday locate your kinfolks."

From his pack, he took a short-handled trench shovel and dug a deep grave. When the body had been covered, he stood beside the grave, bareheaded.

"It's the best I could do for you, old man. I reckon you savvy. So long, R.L. I'll do what I can to find your kinfolks and let 'em know that you died like a man. So long."

He mounted and rode on, the mule following, along the trail of four men, one of whom had done a murder. There was a hard glint in the rider's blue eyes as he rode toward the peaks of the Gila Mountains.

"Biscuits," he broke a thoughtful silence, "what do you reckon brought that boy down here? Not gold, for his hands were too soft to be swinging a prospector's pick. Not cows, for he ain't a cowboy. Men don't follow *El Camino de Chinos* for fun. I'm wondering now, if he didn't die hunting what we came here after? Eh, Biscuits? But why wouldn't we know about him? Tell me that and I'll ask you another."

He broke off in his musing to sweep the country with a pair of high-powered binoculars. The brush had thinned to an occasional Saguaro. Ahead, and a little to the right of the dim trail, lay a shimmering white stretch that, in the heat waves, looked for all the world like a crystal lake some five miles in diameter. In reality it was a mammoth soda bed, white as snow. Across this white spot moved a black speck that danced crazily in the shimmering heat.

"Company, Biscuits. A horsebacker. Angling from out of nowhere in particular, toward this trail. Mebby the guide that piloted the three mariners. Most mebby, though, it's an Indian."

He hid the horse and mule in the brush and watched the approaching horseman through his field glasses. Horse and man took grotesque shape against the stark white background that assumed a mirage-like aspect, tall as a mountain at times, then vanishing completely to appear in another place. Now it appeared like two men and two horses, one high in the air, suspended above the other, vanishing, reappearing.

"A darned clever stunt," mused the watcher. "A man can see him, sure. But he'd play hell hitting him with a bullet. That layer of heat waves offsets his position by many feet. I've handled a surveyor's transit in this country and I know."

When horse and rider did take definite shape and position, the watching man lay aside his glasses and drew his Colt. For the rider was a white man, from his dress. He rode a big-boned gray horse too good for either a Mexican or an Indian. Was he the guide, back-trailing along his route of yesterday? Or was he a cowboy bent on some personal business that had nothing to do with the dark traffic that marked the sands of *El Camino de Chinos?*

The man came on at a steady road gait. He was singing in a careless, resonant baritone.

Oh, Stack O'Lee, he killed a man, over a damned old Stetson hat . . .

CHAPTER
THREE

Not a hundred feet separated the watcher from the watched. The man on horseback was small, sunburned a brick color, and even at a distance had a sort of scarred and battered appearance such as belong to the old-time pugilist. He wore chaps and boots after the cow-land fashion. But his shirt was a rainbow-colored affair of cheap silk, and a checked cap covered his head. The fellow sat his horse well, riding a short stirrup after the manner of men accustomed to an English saddle.

Dynamite chose that moment to fill the desert silence with his loud braying. The glitter of a gun showed in the rider's hand.

Angry as the hidden man was, he grinned dryly at the ludicrous angle of the situation. "Put up that rod, buddy!" he called. "Then keep on coming. You needn't raise your paws but bear in mind that I've got you covered and I'm rearing to shoot you square in the belly."

The rider grunted and, putting away his gun, came on.

"That'll be far enough. Toss that gun of your'n overboard."

The man promptly obeyed. "Now what? Do I sing a song or dance a jig? I ain't crazy about playing tag with no bullet, see, and I wanna smoke before I croak. So ease off me, big boy, ease off."

"Get off and come over in the shade." The hidden cowpuncher came into view, his gun hanging with careless readiness in his hand. The other man obeyed. From under fist-battered brows a pair of shrewd eyes viewed the cowboy. He obeyed the command with alacrity, his movements quick and well controlled. No man but a fighter moves in just that manner — small, compact, a bundle of hard muscle and trained nerves, a pocket edition of a fighter like Bat Nelson, with a shriveled ear and a battered nose. There was a genial grin on the little fellow's wide mouth.

"Hot, ain't it?" The stranger mopped his sweat-streaked face with a soiled purple handkerchief and sat down in the shade, facing the standing cowpuncher. His shrewd eyes watched the bigger man.

"Some hot," admitted the cowpuncher as he squatted on his heels. He looked at the fellow's feet. They were small and, instead of high-heeled cowboy boots, his boots were similar to those worn by jockeys. The cowboy slid his gun back into its holster.

"Thought mebby I'd have to kill you, but you ain't the man I'm after. You can ride along on your way any time. Sorry I delayed you, mister."

"You ain't nutty, are ya, bo?" asked the small man with comical solemnity. "Or hopped up?"

"Nope. I've never done time in a crazy house. Never hit the pipe but once. Made me so sick I never repeated. No, I'm just looking for a man who needs killing."

"Well." The little fellow grinned. "Dat's me, according to de old lady. Ain't it hell how a moll will toin against a guy when de breaks come bad? When I'm pulling down good dough, see, she's for me. I'm stronger'n garlic with her. I'm Spud Shanley, with a good chance at de champeenship. Only I got a louse fer a manager, see, and he crosses me. He touts dis boid for a set-up and I trains on Tijuana beer and cigarettes. And dis set-up makes a bum outta me, no less. Does de old lady put beefsteak on me map? She does not. She gimme de razz. Takes de air on me, see? I meets her at a brawl a week later. Dis set-up brung her, see? I takes one swing at dis guy's button and his friends is still trying ta bring him awake when de bulls takes me away in de Black Maria half an hour later. Because I'm a gent, I don't even sock her once, see? Dat judge takes one long look and gives me de woiks. Throws de whole book at me, see? I'm sixty days older when I kicks de dust of dat Los Angeles boig from me pedals and goes to Tijuana. I was a good jock once, cowboy. Booted plenty winners under de wire. But no more, Mabel. Too much weight. So de best I get is a job swiping, see? When I ain't at the stable, I'm playing suckers. A guy named . . . but never mind de name . . . anyhow, dis wise sucker slips me a roll. He wants it down on Boy Blue, see? Some hophead tells him dis Boy Blue can fly like a boid with one feather in his tail, see? He tells me ta put dis roll on his nose, see? Foist money. And I've seen dis Boy Blue clocked and he's a dog. A dog, brother. A goat. Dat hee-haw hay-burner dat sounded off a while ago can pedal backwards and make dis Boy Blue look like a tramp."

Spud Shanley gathered a mixture of sand, lint, and tobacco from his pocket and sifted it into a wheat-straw paper. One deft twist and the cigarette was made. Striking a match on his thumbnail, he lit the slender smoke and went on. "What do I do? Just what any wise boid'd do, brother. I pockets de roll, see? I'm aiming ta hunt up mister sucker when dat Boy Blue comes in about sundown with nothing but a bum alibi, and give de guy back his jack. I means well. How do I know dat dis Boy Blue is a mud horse? And it's a muddy track. I'm in de bar lapping up a few beers when dis Boy Blue lopes home two lengths ahead of de field. He's a long shot, see, and I've lost dis boid twenty thousand bucks, no less. So when I gits over de shock, I has dis bartender change some twenties into fins and ones. I pads de roll and finds de gent dat thinks he's won. I slips him his jack and blows. He's still looking for me."

The ex-fighter rose with a sigh. But the cowpuncher halted him.

"You didn't finish the story."

"No. He ain't caught up with me. Den de finish is wrote in one woid. Dead. And he damned near wrote her out for Spud Shanley yesterday. How was I ta know he was coming to dis dude ranch where I lands? I'm making ham and eggs schooling polo ponies when he drives up in a swell car, see? I gives dis pony his head and we keeps on going till you stops me. I sees a big lake and rides dat way, but de lake is dat soda flat. Well, mister, I'll be moping along."

"Which way?"

"I dunno. Dat pony is dry. Where's a water trough?"

The cowboy eyed the little fellow with more interest. He now saw that the ex-fighter was hollow-eyed from fatigue, the scarred face had a drawn look, and the battered lips were black and cracked from lack of water. But he had voiced no personal complaint. He spoke only of the gray gelding's thirst. Without a word, the cowboy rose and got a canteen from his saddle.

"Drink slow. A little at a time. I didn't realize you were dry."

Spud Shanley drank. Between sips of the precious water he looked at his horse. The cowpuncher got a large canteen from his pack and, filling his hat, watered the gray horse. When the canteen was empty, he came back to where Spud sat, watching.

"I ain't got a dime on me, mister," said Spud, fishing out a gold watch, "but ya can have dis ticker."

The cowpuncher shook his head. "You'd better come along with me to camp. You'll die out here. It's a tough country on pilgrims. We'll camp at some water holes and take on grub."

"Dat's me. Mister, I'll try ta square dis someday. Do I keep my rod?"

"Sure thing."

Spud Shanley got his gun from where he had tossed it. It was a small-calibered automatic equipped with a silencer, and as they rode on, he took it apart and wiped the sand from it. "What name, cowboy, if I ain't too fresh?" he asked, hiding the cunning in his eyes by averting his gaze.

"Just call me Dave," came the careless reply.

CHAPTER
FOUR

They rode on for several hours, neither man breaking a
weary silence. If Spud Shanley attached any importance
to the tracks of the four men Dave was following, he
gave no sign. It was almost sundown when they camped
at some water holes.

The cowpuncher, as he unsaddled, then slipped the
pack from the mule, kept an unobtrusive eye on his
companion. He had seen a flicker of something in the
eyes of Spud Shanley as they dropped off the mesa into
the arroyo that held the water. There were signs of a
hasty camp there. Some empty cans. The four men had
eaten there, then ridden on. Spud set about gathering
firewood, his little journeys carrying him farther each
trip. Finally he slipped from view. Dave, moving with
swift caution, followed him. He took a position in a
brush patch, from which spot of concealment he could
observe the small man's cat-like movements.

He saw the ex-jockey crouch by a crevice in the rock
and shove his arm into the cavity up under the rimrock.
He gave the appearance of searching for some object
hidden there. Then the hand came out, holding a small
tin box such as those used by smugglers to carry

opium. His fingers were prying off the lid when the cowpuncher's cold voice interrupted him.

"I'll take that box, *hombre*. And I'll shoot you like I'd kill a rat if you make a crooked move."

For a moment the scarred face went white, twisted with fury. Then he rose slowly from his crouched position and held out the unopened box.

"Toss it," suggested Dave grimly. "You're kind of quick at close quarters."

"You win," came the gritty reply, and Spud tossed him the box.

"Don't make any fool gun play," warned Dave, "while I'm taking a look at the box. What's in it, *yen shee?*"

"Coke." Spud's tone was surly and dangerous. "I need it, bad."

Dave nodded. He had known for some hours that the man was a dope addict, that he had been hopped up when they had met, and that the effects of the drug had worn off, leaving him shaky and tortured and dangerous. "I'll give you your cocaine, Spud." He got the box open. Inside were three tiny vials each containing a large dose. Also there was a bit of paper rolled in the form of a tiny cylinder. Dave kept the paper and tossed the watching Spud one of the vials. Then he unrolled the paper.

It contained a long column of figures. The sum of these figures was totaled at the bottom. A look of disappointment flickered in the reader's eyes, but he grinned derisively at the ex-pugilist who had sniffed his ration of cocaine from the tiny vial and was eying the larger man appraisingly. Dave put away the bit of paper and drew his gun.

"I'm playing a dangerous game, mister," he told the smaller man. "I reckon I'd better bump you off for my own safety. Got any reason why I shouldn't kill you? I'm dead onto your racket."

"Gosh," grunted the little hophead.

"Well, Shanley? I've got your rations of hop. Make it snappy."

"You want me ta toin rat and squeal, bo? Go ta hell!" Spud made abnormally courageous by the drug reached for his gun. Dave leaped forward, swung his .45 in a short arc, and its barrel caught Spud across the eyes in a backhand blow that blinded him. Dave picked the automatic from his hand and shoved it into his chaps pocket.

"Now, you damned double-crossing, coke-sniffing rat, squeal or I'll drop you in your tracks. Who left this note?"

"Dey'll kill me, pal, if I squeal," whined the blinking Spud.

"And I'll kill you if you *don't* squeal."

"Hop to it, big boy," snarled Spud with the doped bravado of his kind.

"OK, mister." Dave put away his gun and taking one of the vials, uncorked it and started pouring its white crystals onto the sand. With an animal-like snarl, Spud leaped. Dave blocked a swing, balanced easily in a fighting pose, and his left jab lifted the smaller man from his feet. "Get up, rat, and I'll repeat. Fighter, eh? Fighter, *bah*."

44

Spud, on the ground, saw Dave reach for a second vial of the precious cocaine.

"Don't, Dave, don't throw it away. It's me life, see? I'll spill de woiks."

"No lies, Shanley. Who left you that stuff here at the water hole?"

"Frosty. So help me, brother, dat's de truth!"

"You mean Jack Frost, from Tijuana, Mexicali, Juárez, and along the line? Describe him."

"Tall, skinny, with a knife cut acrost his mug and hair de color uh snow. Frosty, de gambler. Keno McQueen's gunman."

"Who're the three guys with him?"

"So help me, Jack, I dunno. Dat's straight. All I know is dis. De main gaffer gimme a paper, see. He says ride acrost to de water hole and leave it at dis place. Dere'll be me hop waitin' for me. And a note. And a hundred smackers."

"Gimme your note," snapped Dave.

"Dey'll croak me. Frosty'll croak me!"

"Shut up. Gimme that note. Then go on back and start a fire going."

Spud, white-lipped with fear, handed over a cylinder of paper similar to the one in the box.

"You had orders to leave it in this box under the rock?"

"Soitinly. If I don't me name's mud."

The note contained a list of figures, totaled at the bottom. When Spud, cursing and whining, set about making the fire, Dave sat down with a pencil and a little notebook. Into the notebook he copied the figures, then

45

joined Spud. He handed the tin box with its cocaine to the ex-fighter. Then he gave him the two notes.

"Now listen, rat," said Dave. "Here's the notes, savvy? You put one back in the box and shove the box up under the rock. Then you take the other back to where you started from. Nobody but you and I know that we've met. I won't squeal. You'll be cutting your own throat if you say a word about us meeting. Take the note back and get your hundred bucks. This never happened, savvy? Just a dream."

A crafty look crept into Spud's scarred face. He nodded and grinned at his companion. "I getcha, I getcha. Mum's de woid. Say, are youse a dick? A Customs cop?"

"Do I look like a cop?" Dave laughed.

Spud joined him in his mirth.

"You ain't a bad sort, Spud," admitted Dave, his blue eyes appraising the drug addict. "You'd go along fairly straight if you had a chance. Has Frosty got something on you?"

"Enough, pal, enough. He's a tough baby."

"How about McQueen?"

"I never seen Keno McQueen, pal. I ain't never chinned with no guy dat ever seen him. Mebby he lives in Chicago. Mebby he don't live no place. Mebby he's just a name, see? Like a lodge, see? Like de KKK and de Knights uh Columbia. Dis Keno is a gambling game, see? Mebby Keno McQueen is a gambling lodge. See wot I mean? Youse gimme de grip, see? I slips you de grip. We're Keno's pals, see? Frosty's just a right bower outta de deck. He's like a bobtail flush. Not worth a damn without de rest uh de cards ta fill out de hand."

"Where does Jack Liggett fit in?" asked Dave.

"Him and Frosty is pals, see? He's Frosty's boss. My boss, too. Liggett's gotta square me with dat mogul dat drives up yesterday. He gimme a start. I took de hoidles with me eyes shut. Dis gray gelding is a boid. But we was both lost when you showed. Lemme go now?"

"Better eat something."

"I'll do me scoffing at de ranch. I'll plant de note for Frosty and hit de grit."

"You may see me at the Seven-Up Ranch, Spud. You don't know me, savvy?"

"Poifict strangers. So long."

Dave gave him his directions as he saddled up. He watched the ex-jockey ride off, the cocaine in his system acting as food and drink to a jaded body.

Oh, Stack O'Lee, he killed a man . . .

Distance blurred out the song of the rider. The cowpuncher was alone. He took out his notebook and by the light of the fire studied out the coded messages. After an hour's work, he found the key. The numeral 7 was the letter A, 8 was B, 9 was C, and so on. Decoded, the two messages were written out on a clean page torn from the book. The letter from Jack Liggett to Jack Frost, gunman, read as follows:

Keno and girl due here today. Watch for blue-eyed man on yellow horse. Get him. New man working with Sam. Name Lowry. Odd, eh. Watch everybody, including three fences. Somebody has talked too much. Probably R.L. If he shows, blot him out.

The second note was as meaty with news as the first.

Three fences here. Smell something rotten in air. Not so good. Nothing definite. Just a hunch. R.L. showed. Just too bad for him. Hunting here at its best in two weeks. Low on cigarettes.

Carefully Dave absorbed the contents of the two messages. Then he tore the pages containing the maze of figures from the notebook and painstakingly burned them.

He cooked a frugal meal of biscuits, bacon, and coffee. Then he moved camp to a spot several miles distant. When his animals were grazing at the end of their stake ropes, he went back on foot to the water hole and took up a hidden position near the rimrock where Spud had put the message.

CHAPTER
FIVE

A large bunch of wild horses and burros watered at the holes, their tracks obliterating the sign left by Spud and Dave. Crouched among the rocks, Dave waited, hour after hour. He was tired and sleepy and fought off drowsiness with all his power of will. He wanted to smoke, but dared not risk a light. The moon rose, shedding a pale light over the desert. A bunch of antelopes circled the place a dozen times and finally came to water.

At last the click of shod hoofs told the approach of a rider. Dave crouched with his gun in his hand. The man rode up to the water holes and, dismounting, left his horse there and came down the little arroyo on foot. He halted at the rimrock and shoved his arm in under the rock. He found the tin box and its message. Seating himself on a rock, he took out pencil and paper and, with the aid of a small flashlight, decoded the message.

The flashlight revealed the man's face — a lean-muscled, darkly handsome face, clean-shaven save for a carefully kept mustache of small dimensions, twisted and waxed. A pair of black eyes glittered in the light. Once he smiled mirthlessly, displaying a set of white, even teeth. He was a well-knit fellow, about six feet tall, with good shoulders and a narrow waist. He wore fawn-colored jodhpur riding breeches tucked in the fancy tops of high-heeled boots. A white flannel shirt, open at the throat, a leather jacket, black silk neck scarf, and cream-colored Stetson completed his raiment. Around his waist sagged a cartridge belt and pearl-handled gun. Another gun, a Luger automatic, snuggled in a holster under his left armpit.

Jack Frost, killer, snapped out the flashlight and got to his feet. He took a cigarette from a silver case and lit it from a patent lighter. The brief flame showed his handsome face set in a sardonic smile. A picturesque, handsome man, educated, cunning, reputed to be the owner of a string of border gambling dens, he was a sinister figure along the Mexican line. He came and went at will, suspected of a hundred dark crimes that ranged from white-slave traffic and smuggling to plain and fancy murder. Women were fascinated by his suave manner, his dark face, and his mysterious past. Tourists at Tijuana and Juárez were charmed by his amiable guidance about those towns. Society folks, movie stars, writers in search of local color found Jack Frost a sophisticated host, eager to point out the highlights of the border town. Mexicans found Jack Frost a man who complied with even their most trivial laws. His gambling houses paid their tithes, he drew trade, he ran his gambling games and his bars in an orderly fashion. His girls were not allowed to annoy visitors; his employees were courteous. Mexico accepted him with a shrug, a smile, and a sly wink. Immigration and Customs men listened to his jokes, returned his suave smiles, and did their best to trap him. Prohibition officers gave up in frank disgust. All of them hated Jack Frost with a sort of futile enmity. It was darkly hinted that Frost had broken a dozen border officials with his devilish cunning — Frost and the mysterious Keno McQueen. One official, trapped and disgraced, had blown out his brains. Others had disappeared. The Immigration and Customs men would willingly give a year's pay to be able to wipe the black blot of those disgraced men from their records. They would swear those men had been framed and that Jack Frost was the man who did the framing. But prove it? Impossible. Overlook it and let the men go unpunished? With an ignorant public clamoring for the punishment of crooked officials? The inspectors grew more white about the temples, more haggard, more grim-mouthed, and waited for the chance to catch the wily Jack Frost red-handed. There were a few among the ranks of government men, a few recruited from the cow country, who would enjoy swapping shots with the smiling Jack Frost, and this in spite of the proved fact that Frost was a most dangerous man with a gun.

The man with the puckered blue eyes who crouched in the rocks with a naked Colt did not shoot. He squatted there, his weight on his boot heels, breathing a little quickly. He did not even move until Jack Frost had mounted his horse and ridden away. There was a beaten look in his eyes, and his feet dragged like leaden weights as he trudged back to his camp.

The buckskin horse nickered a soft greeting. Dynamite looked up from his grazing, wagged an ear, then went on feeding. The man rubbed the nose of the pet horse, talking to the animal in a low voice. "We found him, Biscuits. We found Jack Frost. We're all done down here for a spell. Most mebby we should've killed this Jack Frost where we found him. He's ornery, pony. He's sent some good men to hell. That boy back yonder, that we planted . . . Jack Frost done that, and done it from behind. He ain't changed much since we knew him, Biscuits. Same eyes, same sneering mouth, same way he had of wearing purty clothes. He changed his name some, and he travels with high-toned company, they say. But his purty boots make snake tracks in the sand, same as always."

He fed a cold biscuit to the buckskin horse. Dynamite now displayed a marked show of sudden affection and was also rewarded with a biscuit.

"Now go to grazing, pardners. We're pulling out, come daylight. We've found out what we came after, and then some. We learned that the hunting was gonna be good down here in two weeks. We're coming back then, Biscuits, and we're declaring open season on a couple of hot sports that are human skunks and worse. He's low on cigarettes, says he. It must be hell, having to kill boys in the back while you're smokes are low. Jack Frost, eh? Well, Jack Frost, the blue-eyed man on the yaller horse is gonna be gone when you pick up his sign."

He lay down without removing his clothes save for boots and hat. His bed was spread in a brush patch, between the mule and the horse, and he slept with his gun in his hand. An hour before daylight he was up and

52

making breakfast, apparently refreshed by his brief two hours' rest. He saddled Biscuits, packed Dynamite, and headed due east.

Two nights later Dave rode into the light of a Mexican campfire near a little village called San Anton, almost a hundred miles due east of Skeleton Bay. San Anton lies about twenty-five miles below the border.

"!Caballeros!" called the American as a dozen swarthy men dropped their right hands on gun butts. They were in the nondescript uniforms of the old-time *Rurale* police, the finest body of fighting men Mexico has ever had.

Colonel Estaban Herrera, when he made out the features of the rider, leaped to his feet, barking: "*Señor Sandborne! ¡El Capitán!*" He stood with boot heels touching, right arm crooked in a salute.

The man on the horse returned the salute with a wide grin, then said: "As you were, Steve."

"Rest, men," was the colonel's quick command to his men, who had snapped to attention when he had.

"Surprised you, did I, buddy?"

Then Dave turned his horse and mule loose. A wrangler hazed the two animals out to where the remuda grazed, while Dave, invited by the colonel, helped himself to wine and food.

"Dave? You! *Madre de Dios*, my frien'. I was expect' someone else, no?"

"No. I'm the bird that's fetching a letter to you. Phony name, that's all. I'm Dave Sandborne for a spell. Cowpuncher. Never laid eyes inside a grammar, savvy.

It ain't hard when you've been brought up on a cow ranch. I'm Dave Sandborne, cowboy. Captain Wallace David Higgins is doing a long hitch in federal prison. He was court-martialed and sent up for accepting a bribe while in command of the Border Patrol. Disgraced. Busted. Worse than dead."

"But if you are in prison, how are you here?" the handsome Mexican colonel gasped.

"It's done with mirrors, Steve." The American grinned. And Steve Herrera, looking steadily into the eyes of the man who had been his commanding officer in France, read a tragedy behind the sparkle of his friend's blue eyes. He did not question further how Wallace David Higgins, West Point, had now become Dave Sandborne, cowpuncher. Steve Herrera was not a curious man when it concerned his friends. His father, *Don* Estaban, had once owned many thousand acres of a grant that included Skeleton Bay and much of the territory crossed by the sinister *El Camino de Chinos*. The son had been educated at the University of Arizona and had enlisted in the U.S. Army when the World War called for Americans. Colonel Estaban Herrera of the Mexican Army became Buck Private Steve Herrera of the A.E.F. A soldier who had long ago learned to obey a command, he came out with a couple of medals and the silver bars of a first lieutenant. He could handle men as well as he could obey a command. Now he was back in Mexico with the rank of a field colonel with a roving commission and a handful of picked men. His exact mission was known only to the War Departments of Mexico City and Washington. A month ago he had received orders to co-operate with a man named David Sandborne. This Sandborne would bring a code letter. Colonel Herrera would extend the *Americano* all courtesies and co-operate fully. And a few weeks later this man with puckered blue eyes had ridden up out of the dusk, mounted on a buckskin horse, followed by a mule that caught the eye of every Mexican at camp. Those men of Mexico are fond of mules.

"Well, I found Skeleton Bay, Steve, and I had the doubtful pleasure of following *El Camino de Chinos*. But they're not using that old trail to smuggle any Chinamen. No fresh sign, anyhow. Three men landed from a rum boat called the *Sally B*. Three *gringos*, savvy? Frost himself met 'em and piloted 'em to a place you probably know about, down in an old volcano crater. I didn't follow. I met a gent called Spud Shanley. Know him?"

"*Sí*. From Juárez." Colonel Estaban Herrera spoke with slight accent, barely noticeable. At the mention of Spud Shanley his dark eyes lit up. "Dave, I know him. Once he was a pugilist and rated as fairly clever. But high life whipped him. He married a dance-hall girl at Tijuana. She finished licking him, poor devil. He was too heavy for a jockey. He was using hop. Pipe, coke, heroin, *yen shee*, marijuana, anything. He fell in with Jack Frost. A good man with a horse, Spud Shanley. Frost sent him over to Liggett when the racing season was over, I think. Anyhow, I learned he was high-schooling some of Liggett's jumpers and pole ponies. He'd sell out his mother when he needs his hop. They keep him on short rations, *sabe?*"

"So I learned." Dave nodded. He was silent for several minutes as he ate hungrily of beans and *carne* and tortillas. He washed down the last of his food with a draft of wine, and rolled a smoke. He smiled a little through the blue haze of tobacco smoke. "I met Jack Frost," he said quietly.

"You . . . you killed him, Dave?"

"No," said Dave. "No, I didn't kill him. His hour hasn't come yet, Steve. But when it does, and if the job falls to me, I'll either take him alive or take him dead."

Colonel Herrera nodded and downed his drink at a gulp. "What are your plans, Dave? We're ready."

"I'll leave my horse and mule here. Get a car to take me across the line and by way of Ajo to Gila Bend. I'll go down the line from there toward Yuma. They tell me that Jack Liggett is hiring dude wranglers for his guest season. With a mustache and some fancy duds, I'll pass for a rodeo cowboy. I'll play the game from there. Nobody but Jack Frost is apt to recognize me and he's handling the lower end of the game, whatever it is."

"*Dios*, man, but you are taking a long chance." Herrera puffed hard at his cigarette. "If you are caught, you die. You will not be the first."

"I'll take one or two with me if I go," said Dave grimly.

"And what of us? What is our move?"

"Lay low for about ten days. Then slip across toward the three craters. You'll be scouring the country for rebels, savvy? I'll get word to you somehow."

"*¡Bueno!*" Colonel Estaban Herrera brightened. He was thinking of the man known as Jack Frost, the most dangerous man along the border — Jack Frost who, before the war, had borne another name — Jack Frost, half brother of Wallace David Higgins.

Because he would readily risk his life for the blue-eyed man who sat wrapped in brooding, bitter silence, Estaban Herrera now made a silent vow to kill Jack Frost and spare Dave the added grief of killing his renegade half brother. Colonel Estaban Herrera refilled the two glasses with red wine. The eyes of the two men met and held like a handclasp.

"*¡Salud, amigo!*"

"Here's how, buddy!"

CHAPTER
SIX

Jack Liggett disliked strangers. He looked at this one with frank annoyance as he drove up in a nondescript flivver that bore a California license plate. The stranger kicked off the switch, pushed back his hat, removed his gloves, and reached for tobacco and papers in what appeared to be a series of unbroken, blending movements.

"I'm hunting Mister Liggett," he announced, pulling a match across the sole of a fancy-topped boot. "Jack Liggett."

"You're looking at him." Liggett hid his annoyance behind his genial smile. Half a dozen guests had eyed the battered flivver and its occupant with a contagious smile of amusement. This cowboy whose face was a little smudged and red had been tinkering with a refractory motor. His bed, saddle, chaps, and war sack were in the rear of the shambling wreck of a car. He removed a beautiful pure white Stetson to fan himself, and the guests and Liggett saw a sweat-dampened mop of hair that looked almost blond from sunburn. He looked about with an approving eye.

White adobe buildings with red-tiled roofs, tall shade trees. He had come through a gateway that let him into a huge patio. There was a long hitch rack where two or three saddled horses stood. Comfortable chairs, home-made and bound with rawhide, were scattered along under a wide arcade. Here lounged more than a dozen men and women in costumes that ranged from the whipcord and tweed of tailored riding habits to flannel and overalls adopted by others of the Eastern paying guests. Here and there squatted a cowboy in picturesque raiment, spinning wild yarns into gullible ears. Sounds of splashing laughter came from the tiled swimming pool beyond the patio. There was a polo field, a target range, commissary, billiard room, a buffet bar with an imported drink mixer. A Mexican string quartet played somewhere. There was a barber chair in the rear of the barroom and a small dance floor. An atmosphere of desert luxury prevailed. There was occasional carefree laughter. This was the Seven-Up Ranch, open to an approved and limited number of guests who paid for such luxuries as showers, good liquor, spotted ponies, cracked ice, good beds, and excellent meals of Mexican or American cooking. No one but a millionaire could afford to spend many days there. It was exclusive and so subtly handled that the guests imagined they were seeing the real primitive and unpolished West.

"You sure got a swell ranch, Mister Liggett. I reckon I'm gonna like it here, if I land a job."

"I'm glad the place meets with your approval," said Liggett, his hard gray eyes probing the stranger. "It so happens, however, that I'm full handed." He was wondering how this man and his battered tea kettle of a car ever got past his outpost. Liggett kept a man stationed a mile out on each road to turn back such specimens of roving humanity.

"You were full handed, mebby, up till an hour ago. One of your boys is laid up with a busted wrist, Mister Liggett. He tried to head me off and haze me back along the road. I knew he was just acting smart, sort of. So I didn't pay him no never mind until he up and took a shot at my tires or at me. The bullet went through the windshield. It scared me so I got kind of rattled and roped him. I busted him kind of rough. When I slacks my dallies off the steering post, he was acting up like a branded calf. Kind of skinned up, too, he was. His shirt got torn where he was dragged over a cactus. Yeah, he was all bunged up. He hit the trail for town."

The cowboy's puckered blue eyes danced with merry lights. Liggett wanted to swear, but, instead, he smiled. The guests had come closer. The cowboy looked with disarming frankness at a girl in riding clothes who was looking over his car. Her hair was reddish brown and her eyes looked smoky gray under the shadow of thick black lashes. She stood out from the other girls like a thoroughbred among scrubby range stock. The cowboy caught the flicker of amusement in her eyes as she examined the car that seemed to droop with a weary air, its leaky radiator steaming, tires sagging, upholstery broken and torn.

"I wouldn't come too close to her, ma'am. She may blow up. She's sure tricky. Tricky, yes'm. I call her Houdini. About the time you think she's hog-tied with short circuits and carburetor colic, or bogged to the dashboard in mud or sand, she just wiggles and snorts a time or two, then kicks loose. So I calls her Houdini."

No flicker of a smile passed his lips, but his eyes were looking into her gray ones, and a sort of comradeship was made in that brief moment. The cowboy became aware of the fact that Liggett was speaking.

"So you crippled one of my best men, then come here after his job, eh?" said Liggett. "Well, my friend, if that sport model conveyance will turn around and get under way without dropping apart, yonder's the gate and it's wide open. Let's see you travel."

"I ain't hired, then? Mister, I can ride anything on the ranch, rope against any man on your payroll, calf tying or trick riding, box, rassel, play a mouth harp, and sing cowboy songs. I've come plumb from Hollywood for a job. I wouldn't've roped that boy only he was drilling holes in Houdini. You mean I ain't hired?"

"I'm not running a museum, if you know what I mean," Liggett was using this method of ridicule to vent his annoyance. "I've got pack horses that will throw you so high that your mustache will be in full bloom when you light. I've got ropers that will make you dizzy watching them. As for boxing or wrestling, we have no hospital in connection with the ranch. Let's see you start this bus and step on it."

"You're the boss."

The cowboy climbed out of the car and took hold of the crank. But the motor would not start. He choked it, spun it, lifted the hood, and tinkered with the motor. The crowd gathered. And, as a crowd will, even when that crowd consists of men who drive imported cars, they voiced sage advice as to the ailments of the motor. The cowboy listened solemnly to each bit of advice, then followed the proffered suggestion. Spark plugs were removed and cleaned. The carburetor came apart and was probed. The cowboy was red of face and rivulets of perspiration trickled down his face. Tools lay on the running board. The hood was off. The timer, various second-hand spark plugs lay about. The carburetor was dissected and lay in a state of collapse.

Jack Liggett was white-lipped with cold, futile fury. The guests were voluble and gay. The girl with the gray eyes sat nearby, an amused little smile on her red lips.

The sun was dropping behind the skyline. And the flivver was a hopeless, dissected wreck. Now came the bleak announcement that some minute part of the carburetor had been lost. "It's a little old dingus that goes through the whoozit and hooks onto that float whoopitoer," came the technical explanation. "Can't no ways put her back into no kind of shape without that there dingus. It must've dropped into the dust. Looks like Houdini is shore hog-tied for once. Now ain't that ornery?" He wiped his hands on a suit of coveralls that had once been white. Across the back of the coveralls, in once-scarlet letters, was printed: **Packard Service.**

The hot-faced and grimy cowboy began a weary search for tobacco. A portly man with graying hair who, in spite of his checked shirt and overalls, could never pass for anything but a banker on vacation, handed over an opened silver cigarette case.

"Shucks, mister, my hands're dirty. Will you fish out one and hand it . . . thanks, pardner. I got a lighter on Houdini but I reckon it's gone haywire on . . . thanks." The banker held the flame of a sterling lighter to the donated cigarette.

"Get that wreck out of here, brother," snapped Liggett.

"But the dingus is lost."

"I'll get the truck to tow you down the road a ways. You can tinker there to your heart's content."

A dinner gong sounded and the crowd dispersed. But the girl with the reddish hair and smoky gray eyes still sat there. Liggett scowled. If only she would go, he would soon be rid of the fellow with his greasy junk heap. But she gave no indication of leaving. The truck roared up and the driver tossed out a tow rope.

"Mister Liggett." The girl rose and smiled up at the scowling rancher. "If you wish to do me a great favor, will you change your mind and hire this young man?" She spoke in a low tone that did not carry to the cowboy who was attaching the towrope to the dead flivver's front axle. "He's really amusing. He plays the mouth harp, too. This place needs comedy relief, as they say in the movies. Here it is. Please. For me."

Jack Liggett shrugged helplessly. "For you, then, Miss Wingate. But I know his type. They're not so good." He smiled thinly and approached the laboring cowboy.

"You're hired. Miss Wingate has persuaded me to put you on." He lowered his voice. "Tow this damned thing out to the dump and burn it. How much is it worth?"

"I paid a college kid ten bucks for it."

"Here's the ten. It's mine now. Jim, tow this mess out to the dump," he told the truck driver. Then he stalked off to the bunkhouse. He halted and called: "What's your name, cowboy?"

"Dave. Dave Sandborne. Some call me Sandy, but back home where my kinfolks . . ." But Liggett had gone into the bar to wash away the bad taste in his mouth with a highball.

The cowboy looked at the girl. In his hand was a bit of metal. He held it out for her inspection.

"The dingus, Dave?" she asked gravely, looking at it.

"Yes'm. The dingus. Had her hid. But I dunno but what I'd've lost, anyhow, if you hadn't taken chips in the game. It was right decent of you, ma'am."

"Perhaps I had a selfish motive, Dave."

"Uh?"

"You said you could ride and rope and fight and play the mouth harp. I could use a man who is gifted along those lines. Especially the fighting and mouth-harp playing. Does loyalty and silence fit in your bag of tricks?"

The smile had gone out of Jill Wingate's eyes. Dave, searching their smoky depths, saw tragedy and a little fear. She was looking at him with mingled hope and appraisal and perhaps, Dave thought, a bit of suspicion. He recalled that coded message to Jack Frost. *Keno and girl due here.* Was this the girl? What girl? Keno McQueen's daughter? She was making a queer request.

There was something sinister and dangerous in her life. But it was hard to believe that this girl with the level gray eyes was a crook. "Ma'am, you've done hired a cowboy," said Dave earnestly.

"There is a sycamore tree half a mile down the creek, a tall sycamore. Meet me there at midnight, after the dancing is over and the ranch is asleep. It's important, and perhaps dangerous. It may mean that I'm letting you in for a lot of danger. Do you still want to come?"

"Ma'am, it'd take a heap to stop me from coming."

"Midnight, then." And she moved away.

"Let's go, feller," growled the truck driver, a burly man who looked as if he might put up an ugly fight.

"Poor Houdini," said Dave, and, unloading his trappings, he got in behind the wheel and was towed to the dump a mile away. He rode back with the driver, who melted at the mention of a drink. Dave took a pint bottle from his pocket and passed it to the driver.

"Liggett is a human tank and he furnishes plenty of stuff to his guests, but he raises hell if us boys drink. Happy days, cowboy!"

Dave, upon his return to the ranch, was guided to the cowboys' bunkhouse by the truck driver. He deposited his bed, saddle, and war sack on an empty cot, and looked about him. A dozen or more cowboys lounged about, surveying the newcomer with curious eyes. Dave's gaze returned their scrutiny. His eyes were mildly curious, no more. Among the men was Spud Shanley, sprawled on a bunk. Their eyes met without a flicker of recognition. Dave found his way to the washroom outside, conscious of the fact that several

65

pairs of eyes had followed his exit with more than mere curiosity.

The washroom was equipped with showers. Dave stripped and enjoyed the luxury of a hot bath and a cold needle shower. A brisk rub and clean clothes left him refreshed and ready for anything.

The dinner gong called them into the cowboys' mess house. A tall cowpuncher with a thin-lipped mouth and beady black eyes took Dave in.

"I'm Sonora Dent," he said bluntly, "Liggett's main rod here. I hear you had a run-in with Slim Clanton?"

"You mean the boy that stopped me along the road?"

"Yeah. Us boys like Slim. Get me?"

"Meaning you don't like me, is that it?" said Dave. "I'm sorry me 'n' this Slim had that misunderstanding, Dent. We both kind of flared up. He opened up with his gun and I roped him. I didn't want to mess up in a shooting scrape, savvy? I did the best I could."

"Well," said the boss, indicating a vacant seat, "there's Slim's place. Fill it." There was a challenge in the black eyes of Sonora Dent.

Dave slipped into the vacant chair. On one side of him was a big, good-natured cowpuncher who grinned at Dave and winked.

"Slim was Sonora's pet coyote, mister," he whispered. "A stool pigeon. We'd orter elect yuh president, secretary, an' bouncer uh the Bury Me Not Society. I wisht yuh'd killed 'im. Beans?"

On Dave's other side sat Spud Shanley, a little fidgety and surly.

"Ya ain't squealin', pal?" he muttered, reaching for the salt.

"No," replied Dave in an undertone.

"Watch Dent, pal. He'll croak ya, see?"

Dave ate hungrily. The food was good and there was lots of it. The big fellow, who introduced himself as Taller Jones, plied him with careless questions. Dave replied in the same careless manner, and was not at all misled by the loud-mouthed jollity of the heavy-set questioner whose pale eyes were like cold, blue lights. Taller Jones was feeling out the stranger in their midst. Dave knew him to be as dangerous as the black-eyed Sonora or the genial Jack Liggett, as treacherous as that man with the gold teeth who sat opposite, as dangerous as the lean-faced man who sat on Sonora Dent's left — as dangerous, in fact, as any of this picked crew of crooks who passed for cowpunchers of honest habit.

There was a fair sprinkling of younger men among the cowboys. They favored bright shirts and neck scarves, huge hats, and inlaid boots. A swaggering, laughing, carefree lot, these younger fellows, and just a little jealous of one another. They rode each day, guiding parties of guests, voicing colorful tales that were more entertaining than truthful, flirting with the girls when the opportunity permitted, and wholly ignorant of the inner workings of the Seven-Up Ranch. A healthy, clean lot of imitation cowboys. Rope spinners, Dave classed them, and so dismissed them as but vaguely connected with the scheme of things.

Sonora Dent, Taller, Goldie of the glittering teeth, and the man they called Cutter, who sat on Sonora

Dent's left and never smiled, these were the wolves of Liggett's pack. Goldie and Taller kept up a running fire of coarse banter. Dent and Cutter talked in low monosyllables, their eyes always shifting toward Dave in flickering, sidelong glances. As for Spud Shanley, the little ex-fighter and jockey, he was a man apart, friendless, a rheumatic bull terrier among a pack of Malamutes and half-grown Newfoundlands. His battered countenance looked surly, his eyes always alert and suspicious, and he ate in silence. Dave felt sorry for the little fellow. He was out of his element, without a friend.

"Watch Dent, Dave," Spud muttered again. "Him 'n' Cutter."

CHAPTER
SEVEN

"The boss tells me," said Sonora Dent when they were back in the well-lit bunkhouse, "that you're handy with your dukes, Sandborne."

"I came here to work, not fight, Dent."

"But you made that crack. Touted yourself for a boxer and wrestler. You jumped Slim and tricked him somehow. He's in town with a bunged-up wrist. A man as tough as you should get a chance to do his stuff. Cutter, here, was Slim's pardner. He'd like to sample your brand of toughness. Fetch the gloves, Taller." Taller agreed with a whoop of glee. A grin spread about the room. Cutter had taken off his boots and was lacing a pair of soft-soled ring shoes.

"I'll second you, stranger," volunteered Goldie, winking at no one in particular.

"Thanks," said Dave, "but I'll pick this little gent with the dished-in face, being as I gotta defend that fool crack I made to Liggett. I was only funning him some."

Dave pulled off his boots and sat on the edge of his bunk, stripping off his shirt. Spud, showing signs of mingled fear and pleasure, met Taller as the big fellow came in from somewhere with a set of badly used boxing gloves. They were five-ounce gloves, glazed with dirt and dried blood.

Spud began some protest as Taller handed him a pair of the gloves.

"Dry up, you runt. Take them mitts."

Spud snarled something about a dirty deal and came over to Dave's bunk.

"Watch Cutter's left, pal," he muttered, as he laced on the gloves. "He's handy as hell, see. And dat left of his is doctored, see? When dey tape his mitts, dey slips in a layer of lead. And dere ain't enough padding in dat mitt to wad a shotgun shell. But his belly's weak. Woik on his belly, Jack." He took Dave's gloves and worked the padding away from the knuckles.

"Time!"

The two men were on their feet. Dave advanced to shake hands. Cutter met the friendly overture with a backhand slap that stung Dave's cheek. Stripped to the waist, the two boxers sparred for an opening. It was plain that Cutter was no amateur. But, on the other hand, he was far from being made of champion stuff. Dave back-pedaled out of his rushes twice, evading Cutter in a rather awkward fashion. Cutter leered at him, and taunted him as he pushed the fighting. Spud groaned as he watched Dave's footwork. Cutter was heavier, had a longer reach, was a past master of dirty fighting, and his left hand was loaded. Dave danced about, blocking, retreating, without trying to hit.

News of the fight had spread over the ranch. Perhaps Liggett had arranged the thing, for the male guests had slipped in and stood about. The burly, thick-necked truck driver, a couple of mechanics, and two or three men in chauffeur uniforms joined the audience. Dave saw them out of the corner of his glances as he slipped away from Cutter's rushes. Some of the crowd was booing him. Spud's face was white and tense as he crouched by Dave's bunk. There was no roped ring. The crowd made a human circle.

"Fight, yuh bum!"

"This ain't a foot race!"

"Ketch him, Cutter!"

"He's yellah!"

Cutter rushed and Dave side-stepped. The movement placed him within a few inches of Sonora Dent. Dent, with a grin of derision, gave Dave a shove. For a moment he was sent off balance. Cutter's left thudded.

Dave went down. Liggett's voice began counting him out. Dave, on one knee, was taking the count. But Cutter's blow had lacked the force of a knockout and Dave, a little dizzy but far from being out, was taking advantage of the count. Looking up under his arm as he kneeled there, he saw a face outside the window, a face white with emotion — the face of Jill Wingate.

"Seven . . . eight . . ."

Liggett, now the third man in the ring as referee, stepped forward as if to hold up Cutter's glove in victory.

"Git back there!" It was the voice of Spud, the ex-fighter, Spud who knew the game and who had somehow read in the beaten attitude of his fighter certain minute details that told him Dave was not the clumsy-footed boob he seemed to be.

Liggett stepped back instinctively. And at the count of nine Dave was on his feet. There was a thin smile on his lips. He no longer danced about. His feet moved like parts of a perfect machine, quick, shifting, never seeming to lift off the floor. He came toward Cutter, grinning, inch by inch, crouched, his body weaving. Cutter, rushing to finish a groggy opponent, was met by a barrage of blows that sent him, covering dazedly, into a clinch.

"Fight, Cutter!"

Dave shoved him away, ducked a swing, and jabbed at the man's jaw. Cutter swung low and Dave caught the low blow on his thigh. Dave's right hook slid past Cutter's guard, smacking against the fellow's ribs. Now began a fight worth seeing. Dave met every move of Cutter's, blocking, jabbing, side-stepping, following Cutter about, slashing his face with those ripping blows that cut like a knife. The gloves were hard from dried sweat and blood, and whenever one of those slashes found its target, it left a mark. Cutter's loaded left missed, time after time.

"Fight, Cutter!"

The heel of Dave's right hand shoved the snarling man out of another clinch. "Foul me again in a clinch, and I'll put out a lamp!" Dave feinted, then sent a left fully into Cutter's face. Cutter staggered a little. Dave's right spatted across into his man's face. Spud, carrying on a pantomime fight, spat through clenched teeth. "Atta boy!" Cutter's left eye was bleeding. In less than three minutes it would be closed. "Look it . . . a champ!"

Cutter tried to fall into a clinch. Dave kept him off with punishing jabs. "Fight, Cutter!"

Shuffling, weaving, bobbing, Dave followed his man about, playing with him, grinning at him, jabbing him at will.

"He may not know a flivver," chuckled one of the guests who had enjoyed Dave's arrival, "but he can handle his hands."

"And his feet," added another fight fan. "He's no boob. Look!"

"And Cutter's a fighting fool, too. Saw him fight more than once. That new chap is a darb. He's got . . . gosh!"

Again Dave's maneuvering had placed him near Sonora Dent. Dent, with a swift look about him, shoved out a foot, a booted foot to which was buckled a long-shanked spur. A swift, tripping motion, and the spur caught Dave above the instep, jerked swiftly, and he stumbled forward, falling. Cutter's left flashed up and Dave went down. So swiftly had it been accomplished that no man saw the trick.

"One . . . two . . ."

"Time!" chorused half a dozen self-appointed timekeepers.

Like a flash, Spud Shanley was in the ring, dragging Dave's semi-conscious form to his bunk. One of the guests lent ready assistance and together they worked on him.

Dave, limp, glassy-eyed, drooped on the edge of his bunk. Spud's cunning fingers ran up and down his spine like an electric current. "Keep back!" he begged the crowd. "Give 'im air. Woik on de kid's legs, Jack."

Dave sat up slowly, his eyes blank. Spud leaned over him, a towel in his hand.

"Can ya hear me, pal?" he whispered in Dave's ear.

Dave nodded.

"Den take a big breath, see? Breathe deep, see? Atta baby."

Dave, lying back against the edge at the bunk, took several deep breaths. Out of that hum of voices, out of that blurred gray film across his brain came clarity. Faces took shape. He could hear words. Spud was slapping a wet sponge in his face. The other man was massaging his legs. Dave sat up, shaking his head to clear his brain. He saw Cutter, lying back on Taller's shoulder, a grin of triumph on his battered face.

Dave was conscious now. His brain cleared. Strength flowed back into his muscles. He smelled the pungent fumes of aromatic spirits of ammonia. The man working on his legs called attention to the ripped sock and the torn instep where the sharp-roweled spur had ripped.

"Here's what tripped him, Liggett. His foot caught on something. I say, that chap's foot is badly . . ."

"Time!"

Cutter rushed in like a snarling bulldog. Dave ducked his left. Cutter's right uppercut smashed Dave's mouth and brought a spurt of blood from his nose. Cutter's head butted under and up, but Dave twisted his jaw to one side and the foul move failed. Deliberately Dave pushed the heel of his glove into

Cutter's face. A grin spread over Dave's bleeding mouth. "Naughty, naughty, big boy!" He rubbed his blood-smeared glove in Cutter's face, then slipped from the clinch. "You must be part goat."

Dave felt stronger than ten men. His feet were light, his muscles tingling with electric co-ordination. He laughed into Cutter's furious face. Dave followed him about, pulling punches that would have laid Cutter low. He moved like a panther, following, punishing, weaving about. He again maneuvered within a short distance of Dent.

"You trip me up again, you dirty snake," he said without taking his eyes from Cutter, "and I'll drag you into the ring and slap you silly. I mean you, Dent."

"What yuh talkin' . . . ?"

Dave swung sideways. His right hand flashed in an ugly swing. It caught Dent fully in the mouth. "Excuse me, my foot slipped, Dent." And as Cutter rushed, he swung his left glove up under that fighter's breastbone. Cutter dropped like a shot beef and Dave, stepping across the fallen man, walked to his bunk. He held out his gloved hands to the delighted Spud. "Take 'em off, Spud. Cutter's got enough, I reckon."

Dave sat down on the edge of the bunk. That feeling of exhilaration was ebbing from him. He felt a little sick and fought off a sensation of dulling faculties. Spud held the ammonia bottle under his nose.

Sonora Dent, his face dark with anger, eyed Dave as he worked over the limp form of Cutter. More than one of the guests were talking about Dave's injured foot and what he had called out to Dent about being tripped.

Jack Liggett came up, holding out a congratulatory hand. "That was neat fighting, Sandborne. Damn' neat."

Dave looked up. Several men were close behind Liggett.

"Take a look at the taping on Cutter's left hand before one of his men beat you to it," Dave said, and got to his feet, pushed his way through the crowd, and, walking over to where Dent was unlacing Cutter's gloves, took the soggy, gloved hand from Dent's grasp. "Take off that glove, Mister Liggett, then untape the hand."

Liggett nodded with a scowl of anger and suspicion at Dent. He took a knife and cut the glove lacing and, as his guests crowded about, unwound the taped hand of the moaning, half-conscious Cutter. Under the taping was a thick layer of sheet lead.

Liggett stood erect, a crooked smile on his face, as he showed the lead to the crowd. "When Cutter comes out of it, Dent, pay him off and kick him off the place. I don't want such men around. Put the skids under the bum." He turned to Dave, bluff geniality written on his face, but something quite different in his cold gray eyes. "Good work, Sandborne. I won't forget what you've done this evening."

Dave, dizzy and weak as he was, caught the double meaning of the words. He looked toward the window. The face of the girl outside was gone.

The guests were trailing toward the door, headed for the bar, Jack Liggett, the bluff and genial host, in their midst. Dave, with Spud Shanley in devoted attendance, made his way to the shower room. Stripping Dave, Spud shoved him under the shower. From a battered satchel, Spud dragged forth liniment and rubbing alcohol.

He rubbed Dave down and fussed over him, muttering incoherently. "A champ! How ya feel, pal? Better, eh? Atta baby! Lemme tape dat foot now. I thought dat boid had socked ya fer de count. But Spud Shanley bars no boids as a handler. I brung ya around, eh? How? A sniff of de snow, pal. Just enough. No more. One sniff of coke and you was good. It was me nightcap, pal, but you was welcome."

"I was hopped up, eh?" mused Dave. "So that's what cocaine does to a man?"

"To you, pal. One pinch, see? Made a champ outta ya. Keep at it, and it'll make ya de lousiest bum in de woild. Don't I know."

"I get you, Spud," said Dave, putting his arm across the little pugilist's shaking shoulders. "It's hell, old kid. You used your night's ration of the stuff to pull me around, eh? Look in my pants pocket. I brought you a few shots. Brought it to bribe you with, Spud. But I don't think I'll need it. I've got a hunch you 'n' me'll get along."

"You said it, pal." Spud's hands dived into the designated pocket. "I'm for ya, Dave. But y'didn't win nutting by dat scrap. Liggett ain't tying no can to Cutter, see? Dat was a grandstand play. If ya ain't goofy, ya'll beat it tonight. Dey'll croak ya, kid."

A man who had been just outside the door of the shower room backed softly away. It was Cutter.

CHAPTER
EIGHT

The tall sycamore stood like some grim sentinel against
the moonlit sky. Dave, waiting for the girl with the
troubled gray eyes, was very careful to keep in the deep
shadow. He was almost certain that a man had followed
him, but, try as he did several times, he could not see
the man shadowing him. He cursed himself for an idiot,
getting into that fight. And he wondered, with no little
apprehension, just what he was letting himself in for
now. That look in the girl's eyes had been tragic and
appealing to his sense of chivalry. She had spoken of
danger, had appealed to his manhood. And he was here
to keep a strange tryst of her making.

On the other hand, there was the grave, desperate
mission that brought him here, a matter of honor — the
honor of the name he no longer used, of Wallace David
Higgins, captain of cavalry and son of a man whose
name was without taint — old Bill Higgins, ex-Texas
Ranger and cowman, who had died before the war,
broken in health and in money affairs. He had died
disgraced by his stepson Jack, who had been cashier of
his bank — Jack Higgins, alias Jack Frost, gambler and
smuggler, son of old Bill Higgins's second wife. Jack
had used the bank's money in speculation. His

78

stepfather had sold the ranch and his herd of white-face cattle to pay off the creditors of his Texas bank. Dave's share of the ranch had also gone to save his father.

Bill Higgins, deserted by his wife, ruined by her son, had stood with his back against the wall, so to speak, facing his enemies who, in fear of losing a few dollars, flung the disgrace of his stepson at him. A white-haired, white-mustached old Texan, with deep blue eyes, facing a mob that called him thief and traitor. So Dave, on a hurried visit home from West Point, had found his father, a grim-lipped, snowy-haired old warrior, surrounded in his own home by a snarling, snapping cur mob. And a **Closed** sign was on the bank door.

Dave did not return to West Point. Shoulder to shoulder with old Bill, he had stayed and fought. He sold the cow ranch that was the old Texan's pride. He paid off the mob, dollar for dollar, with a grim smile on his mouth and an old Colt six-shooter hung from the worn belt around his waist. It was old Bill's gun and belt. And a Ranger captain who remained loyal said afterward that it was old Bill's grin on the boy's mouth.

The stately old home in town had to go. Bill had died in a log cabin down at the old ranch on the Pecos. Dave had stuck by him till the end. And when Bill Higgins, Texan, had been buried near the little old log cabin where Dave had been born, Dave had joined the regulars and gone to war.

All that remained of the Higgins outfit was the original homestead on the Pecos where old Bill was buried alongside the grave of Dave's mother. And when the war was done and Dave was captain of cavalry on border patrol, some sinister smuggler machine had laid its trap and caught the young officer. Captain Higgins had paid the penalty of knowing too much. He had made his section of the border too hard on smugglers. So they had broken him with diabolical cleverness, disgraced, court-martialed, sent to the living death of federal prison, for accepting bribes from the smuggling fraternity.

Yet here he was, free, under a new name, back along the border. And when Colonel Herrera had asked the solution, Dave had grinned and replied: "It's done with mirrors." This Colonel Estaban Herrera, with his picked troopers, now awaited orders. As a man and a soldier, Dave was bound to do his part. He could not be false to that man whose loyalty was a thing to make a man believe again in dreams.

Something moved along the trail. Dave's grip tightened on his gun, then relaxed as the girl in riding breeches, boots, and tweed coat stood beneath the tree.

"Better come over here in the shadow, ma'am," called Dave softly. "You might be followed."

She started a little as the words came out of the dark shadow of the brush. Then she nodded and came to where he waited.

"It was brave of you to come, Dave Sandborne," she said. "I think you are aware of the danger?"

"Perhaps."

"This is no time to beat about the bush," said the girl with alarming directness. "I'm Jill Wingate. My father is Grover Wingate of New York and Chicago. You saw him at the ranch . . . the big man with the bushy gray hair who is with Jack Liggett a lot. We come here once a year. Dad goes into Mexico hunting mountain sheep. He is going again in two weeks, and I have good reason to believe that he will never return alive." She spoke in a voice barely above a whisper. Tense, but calm and steady enough, Dave noticed. "You have a purpose in coming here," she went on. "I won't ask that purpose, but I know it is a desperate task that brings any man, unasked, to the Seven-Up Ranch. I know Liggett suspects you. That fight tonight was forced on you. Take care that they don't crowd you into a gun play and kill you, as other men have been killed. Branson, Carter, Edwards, Waldron, and another who died recently somewhere in Mexico . . . those men played your game and lost. In each case they met death in a manner that left no proof of murder. Keno McQueen is cunning."

"You know Keno McQueen?" asked Dave.

"Only as a name. But Jack Liggett and Jack Frost are his two lieutenants. Sonora Dent, Cutter, and these others are lesser dangers. I doubt if they're trusted with the actual killings, but watch them. They're bad enemies. Cutter may take the responsibility of personally killing you. Liggett gave him a terrible lacing because he blundered this evening, and Dent came in for his share of the fireworks, so be careful. Jack Liggett suspects you. If you could overcome his suspicion, he would put you to a test, and if you passed that test, he'd hire you as one of his killers. He'd give a lot for another man like Jack Frost. There's a million in it for the right man, if he succeeds. If he fails, his wages are death. His life against a million dollars. Not a bad gamble for a man of desperate courage."

Jill Wingate's eyes searched Dave's for a long moment, there in the dusky shadow. She stood close to him, so close that the fragrance of her hair filled his nostrils. He could hear her breathing and somehow he knew that she was trembling. His blood pounded through his veins and into his throat. When he spoke, his voice was husky.

"And the job of Liggett's?" he asked.

"The job comes only after you've been tested. The test comes first."

"And what is this test?" Dave asked, trying to quiet the eager tremor in his voice.

"The test is to take me prisoner and hold me down in Mexico."

"*Hmmm*, and why does Liggett want you kidnaped?"

"Because I know too much about *El Camino de Chinos*. I might spoil their plans. So I'm to be taken prisoner and kept down there temporarily or, if necessary, permanently. That is the test, the first part of some man's job."

"And the rest of the job?"

"Is simple enough. You murder my father."

"I understand now," said Dave grimly, "why the job would be worth a million. Grover Wingate is a multimillionaire and a big man in politics. You're his daughter. The man who does the job will need a million to get beyond the reach of the law."

"Yet there are men who will take the gamble . . . Jack Frost or Sonora Dent or Cutter."

"But if you and your father know of this plot, why do you stay here?"

"My father doesn't know. They don't suspect that I know. And to save my father's honor, perhaps his life, and my own life, I must stay here. I must play out the game, to the very end."

Again she paused, like a runner whose strength is spent. She swayed a little, and Dave, finding her hands in the darkness, felt them cold as ice.

"And so I beg of you," she went on, her voice a broken, pitiful whisper, "to accept Jack Liggett's offer, if it is made. I will go with you, do what you ask of me, give you my body and my soul and my life, if you will spare my father. I will see that you are paid as well as Jack Liggett or Keno McQueen can pay you. I will go with you anywhere and for always, if you will spare my father's life. You are not a murderer or a craven coward or a criminal. I am a woman and I know a man, a real man, when I meet one. I am not trying to flatter you, though I would if I thought it would help. I am begging you for mercy. I am desperate. God in heaven only knows the depths of my despair. I am appealing to your chivalry, your manhood, to the love you bear your mother or sister. And I am asking you to risk your life for a man you do not know and a girl you may despise."

Dave's arms went about her quivering shoulders. Without passion, without any emotion save that of pity, he held her as she sobbed brokenly, terribly, her face hidden against his shoulder. "You're taking this too much to heart, Miss Wingate. If Liggett will give me the job, I'll kidnap you and place you in safe hands. I'll give you my word as a man, and swear by all that a man honors I'll do everything that's humanly possible to save your father. As for pay, all I want is the pleasure of smashing Keno McQueen and his jackal tribe as they have smashed other men. I came here to do that job. If I can be of assistance to you, I'm only too glad of the . . ."

Dave broke off suddenly. His eyes, fixed on the trail to the ranch, had seen a shadow move, not a hundred feet away, a furtive, swiftly moving shadow, then a second shadow, following. Now, even as his arms tightened protectively about the girl, and his gun hand slid his Colt from its scabbard, he saw the flash of a gun, a spurt of red flame. But there was no report, only a dull, muffled *thunk* and the crash of a falling body. A man, using a gun equipped with a silencer, had shot another man.

"Don't shoot, pal! Don't shoot, champ! It's me, see?" And Spud Shanley came toward them with that quick, light-footed gait of a boxer. "Excuse me for a bum, champ," he panted huskily, pulling off his cap. "Dat boid, Cutter, was stooling on ya, see? I had to hoit him. You was decent to me, Miss Wingate, and de champ here stands with me like me own brudder, see? Cutter was gonna spill wot he hoid. I had to croak him."

CHAPTER
NINE

The Seven-Up remuda came down off the horse pasture on the mesa. Dust from their coming rose in a gold-dust haze across the rising sun. It was one of those still, cloudless mornings when the ragged peaks of the Southwest rise out of the dawn like the great shrine of a vanished people, beautiful, awe-inspiring, misty with vastness. Somewhere a wolf howled, and, quitting its night's kill, slid off among the rocks to its den to sleep.

The cowboys waited at the corral to rope out the horses for the day's work. The remuda swarmed through the gate, which was swung shut. Goldie, Taller, and Sonora Dent caught out circle horses. They worked with the cattle and had no time to waste with dude guests. That more pleasant but less skilled task was for the rope-spinners.

"Snare that bald-faced black with the stockin' laigs, Sandborne," Goldie ordered.

Dave nodded. He stood, with several others, in the center of the milling bunch of horses. He flipped a loop in his reata and, with a backhand throw, made a neat catch, whereupon the bald-faced black gelding snorted and leaped forward. Two cowboys helped pull the horse to a whistling, stiff-legged halt.

"War Bonnet is kinda snuffy of a mornin'," chuckled someone.

"It'll rain cowboys afore long," said another.

Dave went down the taut rope with his hackamore. Even a green hand would recognize War Bonnet for a spoiled bronco. Twice the black gelding struck wickedly with his forehoofs. Dave ducked the striking death and grinned crookedly at Goldie.

"Front hoof that horse before he gits the remuda choused up and the ridin' master gits his face mussed up!" called Sonora Dent.

Goldie snared War Bonnet's front hoofs. "He's a trick horse, this War Bonnet. He's bin learned to shake hands."

Dave got the hackamore on his head and led the horse out of the main corral, and into a smaller one that was empty. Beyond the small breaking corral was another where Spud Shanley had corralled his high-school horses. Spud did his own wrangling and was puttering around in the corral with half a dozen nose bags filled with grain. He hung the bags on his horses, calling them by name as they came up to him with feigned timidity, like so many coquettes.

Spud made no offer to aid Dave. This had been discussed the night before after Jill Wingate had left the two together with the dead body of Cutter. Spud had told Dave that Dent would probably give the newcomer the outlaw War Bonnet, a man-killer that had thrown the best of the Seven-Up bronco twisters. The two had decided that Spud had better not show his friendliness. It would arouse suspicion. Someone would find the dead body of Cutter who lay in a twisted heap along the trail, a jammed automatic in his hand and a round black hole between his eyes. Yes, it was better that Spud and Dave did not appear so chummy.

So Dave and the man-killing War Bonnet fought it out alone. Dave got the saddle on him and turned him loose in the corral, then he joined the group that were following the call of the breakfast gong.

"If you're scairt of that black pony, Sandborne," Sonora Dent said in a tone that carried the length of the breakfast table, "turn 'im loose and ketch a dude mount."

"I wouldn't cheat you outta your fun, Dent, for anything," replied Dave flatly. "I told Jack Liggett I'd ride any horse that wore his iron. If I can't sit this War Bonnet horse, Dent, I'll roll up my bed and quit."

A ripple of comment swept the table. Not a few grins and nudges passed along the line of cowboys.

"By the way, Dent." Dave smiled thinly at the foreman. "Before it slips my mind, your fighting man ran up against some hard luck last night. I mean Cutter. He's down the creek near that lone sycamore. You better send somebody down there before the buzzards get to him."

A hush dropped over the table. The eyes of every man were fixed on this stranger with the puckered blue eyes. Dave never took his gaze from Dent's swarthy face.

"What the hell yuh pullin' on us, mister?" sneered Dent.

"I'm pulling nothing unless I'm crowded, Dent. Then I aim to pull a gun and I'll pull it damned fast. And when I use that gun, I'll demonstrate the difference between fooling and shooting. That goes as she lays. Cutter jumped me as I was taking a little stroll in the moonlight. I shot him plumb between the horns."

"The hell you did!" gasped Sonora Dent.

"I'm peaceful by nature and inclination, mister," said Dave in a flat monotone, "but I'll fight if I'm crowded. I'm warning you to let me alone, that's all. I'll ride that black gelding or hit the road for town. And Mister Sonora Dent, I'll fight you any time, any place, any way that you want. That's my bet. Call it now or else leave me alone. Put up or shut up."

Sonora Dent, his dark face a shade pale under its heavy tan, looked down the table and into a pair of the coldest eyes he had ever seen. The foreman's right hand was below the edge of the table, out of sight. That hidden hand gripped a gun butt. A challenge had been flung at him. There sat the man who had hurled that challenge, cool, tense, smiling a little, but with eyes as cold and blue as new ice. "I'll call that bet, Sandborne, don't worry. But I'll take my own time and pick another place than this. I don't want to git canned fer killin' some loco fool in the mess hall. It'd give the place a bad name. But don't worry, brother, I'll call your bet and when I call, I'll open the pot with six aces." His lips twisted in a sneer. "Six round, hard, soft nose aces, caliber Forty-Five."

Dave nodded and grinned. "Any time, Dent. Any place. I'm your huckleberry. I knew you were yellow as hell the minute I looked at you. You got your hand on a gun now, but you lack the guts to pull it. Because, Dent, if you make the mistake of drawing that rod, I'll plant a bullet right in the center of your belly. If I was you, and was rodding an outfit, I'd fight or I'd quit my job. You played me a dirty, low-down trick last night. You ain't man enough to back up the play. I'm calling you now, Dent, with your men listening to every word. My hands are both in sight. You've got the edge on me. But you won't pull that gun because, if you do, I'll kill you. You . . ."

"That'll be about enough of that line of gab!" Jack Liggett's big frame darkened the doorway and his voice, big and sonorous, filled the mess hall. Behind him stood two men in the olive green uniform of the Immigration Service. "If you boys must fight, get off the ranch to do it. Sandborne, drop around to my office when you're through breakfast. Dent, here are two hungry men. You already know Sam. Shake hands with Tex Lowry, his new partner. See that the cook gives them the best we have." He turned to the Immigration men. "Dent, here, will fix you boys up."

The two Immigration men found empty seats. Tex Lowry took Spud's place. For some reason Spud had not come to breakfast.

Again the hum of conversation passed the length of the table. Taller had made some remark of coarse humor, and they laughed a little hysterically as men will when they have just looked at something grim and

89

deadly. Dave went on eating. He had hoped to crowd Sonora Dent into an open gun play. He had nursed no intention of killing Dent. But he wanted to smash that gentleman's gun arm with a heavy lead slug, thus cutting down the fighting force of Liggett and Keno McQueen. And likewise he wished to get into the good graces of Jack Liggett. Liggett was on the look-out for a desperate fighting man, a killer. Dave was after that job, and he was willing to cripple the gun arm of Sonora Dent in the process of qualifying. He wondered what Jack Liggett would have to say to him. Dave, barely tasting his food as it went down, ate heartily. He paid little notice to the Immigration officer at his side.

But if Dave paid little heed to his table companion, that indifference was not contagious. For Tex Lowry was showing a marked but vital interest in Dave. Tex Lowry and his partner had heard Dave's low, vibrant voice as it cut through the hush of the mess hall. They were more than merely curious to see what sort of man hurled that challenge of death. And they had seen a handsome, tanned, pleasant-looking cowpuncher with puckered blue eyes who smiled at a man who bore a hard reputation as a gunfighter. There were three notches on the handle of Sonora Dent's gun. Tex Lowry's interest in the blue-eyed cowpuncher had suddenly assumed a more marked tensity. He was staring at a ring on Dave's finger, a seal ring marked with the initials R.L.

Lowry's jaw muscles tightened and his eyes were hard slits. But he said nothing until he had gained perfect control of his emotions. "When you have time," spoke Tex Lowry in a very low tone, "I'd like a word with you."

"With me?"

"With you," replied Tex Lowry in almost a whisper. "Alone."

"There's a black bronc' in the little corral," replied Dave, dropping his voice and passing a bowl of oatmeal as if it had been asked for. "Meet me there." Dave was wondering what new complication would now arise to increase the difficulty of his position. Did this Tex Lowry suspect his mission here? Was Lowry in league with Jack Liggett? Dave gave up the problem and left the table.

Dent gave him a sneering, sidelong glance as he passed out. Dave crossed to the room across the large patio that served Jack Liggett as an office. One or two guests were stolling about but the majority of them were late risers and not yet astir. Liggett looked up as Dave entered. There was an enigmatic smile on the ranchman's wide mouth.

"Shut the door, then sit down, Sandborne."

Dave obeyed, taking care, however, not to turn his back on the big rancher. Men have been killed for being careless about such details. This precaution did not escape Liggett and his eyes were glinting with a grisly sort of humor as he waved Dave to a seat, where the light fell squarely into the cowboy's face. Liggett's face was somewhat hidden by the shadow and the tilted brim of his huge Stetson hat.

"There is an expression sometimes used, Sandborne," Liggett's suave voice broke the silence, "to describe the position of a man whose life on earth is so insecure that it's a matter of luck regarding his survival. We say of such a man, that he 'is on the knees of the gods.' That about fits you. Come clean with me. What's your racket?" Liggett leaned forward, his cold gray eyes like two pinpoints of white fire.

"Meaning?"

"Meaning, my versatile *amigo*, that you came here with a set purpose. You stalled that flivver on purpose. You were overheard to say that you intended bribing Spud Shanley. You fought Cutter, proving that you are no common cowhand but a skilled boxer. This morning, as I took my usual early ride, I came upon the dead body of friend Cutter. And a few moments ago I heard you challenge Sonora Dent in no uncertain terms. In fact, you have all the earmarks of the man who has just joined the Suicide Club. You're not drunk. You don't look like a hophead. If you're a detective, you're a poor one. You don't look loco. Now what's the racket, brother?"

"Well" — Dave grinned — "I kind of got off on the wrong foot at the start. I wanted a job. I made some fool brags, hoping to get put on. Now that I built me a tough rep, I've gotta go on living up to it. Cutter was out to get my taw. I beat him to it. Your man, Dent, being fond of Cutter and that Slim fellow I roped, is raring to kill me. I read Dent's sign and called his hand. The same goes for Taller and Goldie if I stay here and they crowd me. I didn't come here to jangle, but I don't aim to be run off the place like a coyote. It's up to you to fire me, Mister Liggett."

92

"And supposing I don't choose to fire you?"

"I'll hang and rattle till Dent or one of his pardners gets me, that's all. I ain't running off like no coyote."

"*Hmmm*. I see. Now let's look at it like this. You killed a man last night. If I care to push the matter, a jury of twelve men will give you life. Perhaps hang you. Not so good for you, eh, *amigo?*" Liggett smiled dangerously. "Not so good."

Dave shrugged. "Your money could sure put me away where I wouldn't have to worry about board and room, all right," he agreed.

"Exactly. I knew you'd get that point. Brother, I can send you up for the limit. Or I can kill you where you sit and come clear. You're not monkeying with Sonora Dent now. My hands, as you see, are in my pockets. One of them is holding a gun. I can croak you and not even go to jail for an hour. You made enough talk at breakfast to clear me. Do I make that point clear?"

"You sure do, Mister Liggett. Now let's have your proposition. You've got one, or I'd be under arrest right now. Spread your sougans and I'll hunt 'em for lice."

Dave grinned through the cigarette smoke into Jack Liggett's cold eyes.

"All right. I'll spread the cards on the table, Sandborne. Play your hand right, and there's a million in it. Welch the bet and you'll never live to see another moon. Get that?"

"I surely do."

"There is a young lady at this ranch, the lady who persuaded me to hire you. Now I'm quite fond of this young lady but the affection is not what one might term mutual. Get me?" Dave nodded and Liggett went on. "Now, if that young lady were to find herself in grave danger, a danger from which I rescued her, she might find me a more likeable sort. Say I give you the job as her personal guard. She likes to ride alone around the hills but her father and I know the danger to a woman alone and insist on a guide for her. You and she will ride across the line to a certain spot in Mexico, not far below the border but to a place that no man around here knows. You will keep her prisoner there for a period of two weeks or so. You will send out letters asking a big reward. That money will be paid you. It will be yours without reservations. But you will not give up the girl. You'll leave her a prisoner at this spot I name. I'll ride down there and rescue her. You'll have the money. I'll have the girl. And no harm done anyone." Liggett paused, smiling warily. "Want the job, Sandborne?"

"How much is in it?" countered Dave, wondering what the real game was.

"Half a million in currency, paid in Mexico, and a clear trail for you to get away. It'll be to my advantage to have you quit the country and never return. In fact, that's part of the contract. This climate will cease to be healthy. There's the matter of poor Cutter, understand? His friends would be glad to tie a hangman's knot around your neck. Yeah, Sandborne, half a million. If you handle the job neatly, I'll put you in the way of making another half million."

"That's big money, mister." Dave grinned.

"It's a big job." Jack Liggett nodded. "I need a man with plenty of sense, ingenuity, tact, and guts. I've had an eye on you. You are no common cowhand, but that's your business. Do the job and you get the money. Try to double-cross me and you'll go out like a candle in the rain. For your sake, *amigo*, I hope you're not one of these silly government dicks trying to sniff *yen shee* and chink tracks along *El Camino de Chinos*."

"I'm no government dick." Dave smiled crookedly. "When do I start?"

"This morning. I'll speak to Miss Wingate. Her father and she have both fallen for your line. Here's an envelope that you'll open after you cross the line. It has a map of the place where you'll go. You'll find a cabin stocked with all kinds of grub. Also there's a couple of guns cached there. The Mexican on duty at the border will pass you across without further passport than a letter I'll give you. You're taking Miss Wingate to show her some old extinct volcanoes."

"About these ransom letters," asked Dave, "and the reward?"

"The ransom letters are with the map, numbered in their order. I'll send Spud Shanley with the reward money."

"Good." Dave rose from his chair.

Liggett smiled and was about to shake hands when Jill Wingate passed by the window. The rancher hailed her with his big voice. She came into the room, a boyish figure in riding clothes, fresh from a shower and breakfast, but looking tired and strained.

"Dave Sandborne here is familiar with the lower country, Miss Wingate. I've assigned him as your personal guide, as he seems to be the proper sort of man for the job. You wish to take a look at those old craters?"

"Yes, indeed." Her smile seemed forced and her eyes were shadowed with tragedy. "Could we ride there today?"

"If you don't mind riding back by moonlight." Liggett's eyes held hers for a brief moment. In his eyes glittered a sinister warning; hers held only pain and fear. If Dave saw that brief glance, he gave no sign.

"I'd love it." She pretended an animation that did not deceive Dave, who pitied her with all his heart. "My horse is saddled and ready."

"So is mine." Dave grinned wryly. "Sonora Dent staked me to a sure enough ridge runner. His name is War Bonnet."

"Dent takes a little too much responsibility around here," snapped Liggett. "Tell him I said to give you Traveler."

"That War Bonnet looks to me like a real animal, Mister Liggett," said Dave. "Don't know when I've seen a likelier horse."

"I paid enough for the brute," said Liggett, "but he's a spoiled horse. No man ever sat him long enough to warm a saddle. He's crippled several men. I've been thinking about shooting the black devil."

"When I came here," said Dave, with a return to whimsical humor, "I made the crack that I could ride any horse on the place. I'll try that War Bonnet pony. In

96

fact, I've gotta ride him. The boys at the corral are expecting it. What'll you take for the horse?"

"Ride him," said Liggett sourly, "and I'll make you a present of him and throw in his pedigree. He has one a foot long."

"I call the bet." Dave dusted imaginary specks from his snowy Stetson. He suddenly remembered Lowry, the Immigration man. Fearing Lowry might have an inkling of his reason for being here and realizing the danger of being seen in private conversation with a government man, Dave sought to forestall disaster. "Mister Liggett," he said, including the girl with his eyes, "there's a man at the corral that's right anxious to ask me some mighty personal questions. This feller is an Immigration officer. I don't exactly know what his game is, or what he aims to do, but he had a bad look in his eye when he said he'd like a few words with me alone. It may be that I'll be moving kind of fast when I ride outta that corral. Savvy?"

"I get you, Dave," Jack Liggett said, laughing and winking broadly. "Is it Lowry, you mean?"

"That's the gent."

"I wondered what brought him here so early in the morning. What's your plan, Dave?"

"Supposing Miss Wingate starts out now. I'll catch up with her along the trail."

"Good enough." Liggett chuckled. "I'll be around the corral when you start, Dave." He handed Dave a large, bulky envelope that Dave pocketed.

"We'll meet along the trail, then?" asked the girl, looking squarely at Dave, her eyes a little suspicious.

"Yes, ma'am. And if Mister Liggett would kind of make arrangements to have a couple of tires on Lowry's car go flat, I'd be obliged."

Liggett's heavy chuckle followed Dave and the girl outside. She walked with him as far as the hitch rack where her saddled horse stood.

"Aren't you overplaying your hand a little?" she asked, a chill note of suspicion in her voice. "That being followed here by Lowry sounds queer, but Jack Liggett ate it up without a highball to wash it down. But be careful. Remember, I'm depending on you, Dave."

She gave him a long, rather scrutinizing look, then swung easily into her saddle and was gone.

Dave watched her ride out through the huge gateway onto the trail. Then he went toward the corral to ride War Bonnet, the man-killer.

CHAPTER
TEN

A crowd lined the top log of the round corral. Dent, Taller, and Goldie sat side-by-side. Guests and dude wranglers were passing gay banter. Half a dozen girls and a few matrons had come to watch the black gelding throw its rider. Lowry and Sam sat a little apart. As Dave came toward the corral, his chaps hung over his shoulder, Tex Lowry climbed off the corral as if to intercept him. But Dave was too crafty to be caught. He slipped through the gate and into the corral where War Bonnet trotted about, stirrups slapping gently, hackamore rope dragging in the dust.

"*What the devil does that fellow, Lowry, want of me, anyhow?*" mused Dave to himself as he stood in the corral, buckling on his chaps.

Spud Shanley and two young cowboys squatted on their heels inside the corral, ready to help with the horse. With a deft move, Dave stooped and caught the long hackamore rope of braided horsehair. War Bonnet, as the rope went taut, swung about, braced with stiff legs, whistling through red nostrils.

Dave grinned admiringly at the splendid animal. Dust covered its sweaty coat. Dave saw now that this horse was far beyond the ordinary range horse in matter of breeding. Of Arabian strain, it was as perfect a saddle horse as the mind and dreams of man could conjure up in terms of speed and beauty and endurance. There was no trembling of fear in the clean limbs, no inbred white in the eyes that blazed so redly. Here was a horse that stood with a splendid courage, ready to die fighting against mankind.

Waving the other men back, Dave went about the dangerous task of handling the animal alone. Time after time, he worked his way down the rope, talking softly to the horse. Each time he was met with an attack of flinty hoofs. The crowd became restless. Taller was making sarcastic remarks in a rather flamboyant tone.

"That hoss'll be played out by the time yuh git on 'im!"

"Where's your sugar, bronc'-peeler?"

"Sprinkle salt on his tail, cowboy."

"Spare the quirt and use kind words, says the feller."

But Dave paid them no more heed than if he had not heard. Liggett now took his place beside Tex Lowry and Sam.

Dave at last got to the head. A moment later his heavy silk neck scarf covered War Bonnet's eyes. Spud grinned expert approval as Dave stooped and unbuckled his spurs. After a few uncertain jumps, the blindfolded horse stood there, quivering now with a spasm of terror. Dave, without the usual preliminary of cautious stirrup-twisting and cheeking, swung into the saddle.

He felt War Bonnet squat as his weight settled in the saddle and his foot went into the right stirrup. Then,

100

leaning across the sweaty neck, Dave pulled off the blindfold. A tense moment as the black horse trembled under him. Dave felt the muscles of the horse grow taut. Then, with a squeal of rage, War Bonnet leaped. The show was on.

Pitching, twisting, sun-fishing, swapping ends with a jerk that seemed to break the rider's spine. Dave, white-lipped, cold-nerved, clear-eyed, sat his saddle and made no move to halt that desperate spasm of pitching. He rode clean, trying to anticipate those lightning-swift twists and slants. His hat was in his hand but he did not fan at the lowered head. Nor did he rake the sides of the pitching horse. He wore no spurs. His quirt was hung on his saddle horn. He was sitting on the hurricane deck but without a flourish or gesture of bravado. He simply rode a wicked bucking horse that was trying every trick in its cunning brain to unseat the rider. It became a test of endurance, rather than a fight, as if some strange understanding existed between man and beast.

Blood trickled from Dave's nose. The jolting made him sick with aching nausea. He was utterly tired, his body racked with the jolt and strain of the pitching. But he felt the weariness of defeat in the movements of the black horse. A tense silence held the crowd. They had never seen such a horse, or such a rider. Even Taller's mouth grew silent with respect. Liggett's gray eyes were lit with admiration for the man who sat so well in the pitching saddle. And when War Bonnet, after a final desperate fit of pitching, threw up his head and trotted sullenly around the corral, a faint but sincere cheer greeted the exhausted rider.

Around the corral a score of times Dave went, until he felt dizzy and nauseated. But the black horse was getting back his wind and strength.

"You win, Dave!" called Liggett. "I'll stand pat. War Bonnet's yours. Get off and rest a while."

But Dave shook his head. Spud was collecting some bets from the younger cowboys. He grinned up at Dave as horse and rider approached him.

"Open the gate, Spud," Dave told him, his voice husky. "Snap into it, *pronto*."

Spud obeyed, wondering if "de champ" had gone loco. The big gate creaked open. War Bonnet saw it through red-filmed eyes. With a rearing lunge, he quit the corral and stampeded for the haven of the open country. Dave turned in his saddle, waving his hat in unmistakable farewell.

"Where's the fool going, Liggett?" snapped Tex Lowry.

"From where I'm sitting," said Jack Liggett with a grin, "he seems to be headed for old Mexico and due to reach Mexico City before schedule time."

"*Pronto*, Sam!" snapped Lowry. "Never mind why. We got to catch that *hombre*."

But when they reached their car, they found two flat tires. A nail had been driven through casing and tube.

"What's he wanted for, Lowry?" asked Liggett as the Immigration man stood, cursing softly. Sam was looking with dumb bewilderment at his new partner, mutely seconding Liggett's question.

"I want that man for murder," snapped Lowry. "He's an escaped convict, one of McQueen's men. Get me a horse, Liggett, and be damned sure it's a good one. I'm going after that crook if I have to follow through the gates of hell to get him. If I thought you'd helped him, I'd send you to jail."

"Dave Sandborne a murderer?" Liggett was thinking just then of Cutter, whose body had vanished as if by magic at Liggett's secret order. "You're positive, Lowry?"

"I was in El Paso when he was sent up for twenty-five years. I'd know his eyes and his voice anywhere. He's an ex-Army officer, cavalry captain. His name is Wallace David Higgins. Now get me a horse, Liggett."

"Brother," said Jack Liggett in a voice that was cold with dangerous sincerity, "if that man is Captain Higgins, I'll give you ten horses and plenty of men to help get him. Damnation! Higgins!"

His big frame was trembling with fury as he gave Sonora Dent swift orders, then sought out the father of Jill Wingate.

"You look like you'd seen a ghost, Jack."

"Ghost? Worse than that. I've seen Captain Wallace Higgins."

"Are you drunk, Jack?"

"I'm not drunk. But you are either blind or else you're double-crossing me, Wingate. Our fighting cavalier, Dave Sandborne, is the former Captain Higgins. I thought you said you were in El Paso and saw him go to Leavenworth Prison?"

"I saw him leave El Paso under heavy guard. But Higgins had dark hair and was clean-shaven and ten years younger than this Sandborne."

"So he bought a bottle of peroxide and bleached his hair. He grew himself some hair on his lip. And so he fooled the keen eyes of Keno McQueen, the cleverest . . ."

"Cut it!" Grover Wingate's face went white as chalk. "Cut that Keno McQueen stuff. And use another tone when you talk, Liggett, alias Big Jim Brady, or you'll find yourself in Sing Sing again and nobody to spring you from stir. Keno McQueen is dead."

"Dead from the neck up," growled Liggett. "What a mess."

"If that man is Higgins," said Grover Wingate, scowling, "he can't do much harm. Send word to Jack Frost. Put Sonora Dent on his trail. They'll pull a squeeze play and get him, that's all."

Jack Liggett opened his mouth as if to speak, then his jaws snapped shut.

"He was to take Jill down to the craters today," Liggett said lamely. "He sent her ahead, along the trail. Another idea of your invention, Keno. To get her out of sight for a while. The map and the ransom letters are in his pocket. I filled him up with that cock-and-bull yarn we made up. Damn it all, that girl of yours will ruin us yet. She's too smart to allow loose around here. Why didn't I play this alone?"

"Because, my dear chap, you lack the brains to put it across. Jill can take care of herself. Dent's gone after him?"

"I sent Dent and Taller and Goldie. Lowry's bent on trailing him. Our boys wouldn't cross that border for a million but this Lowry fool may get him. I can't figure why Lowry's so keen on getting him. *Whew*, he was hot."

"Well, Jack," said Grover Wingate, once more the dignified and esteemed man of affairs on vacation, "I think we have little to fear. Jack Frost is down below. Get word to Frost to take care of Higgins. Send Shanley down right away. And the elusive Captain Higgins will find himself in a tight situation. Let's have a drink. Then we'll send Frost a note by Shanley."

Jack Liggett took three drinks before he sent for Spud Shanley. The big rancher was worried. The dude wranglers were riding away with their parties. An air of uneasy quiet hung over the place, like an invisible pall. Jack Liggett paced the room like a caged animal. Grover Wingate sat in black silence, sipping a highball. Together they watched Spud Shanley ride away toward the blue peaks of the Mexican border. They were alone in the barroom.

"How did Higgins get out?" asked Liggett for the tenth time.

"Now *I'll* ask one," snapped Wingate. "What was he doing down by the lone sycamore last night? And why didn't we hear the shot that got Cutter? And why is Lowry after him? I can ask some more just like those. All we can do is lay low and hope somebody cuts Higgins down and does it quick. If he tells Jill what he

105

knows, I'm sunk. She'd rather see me dead, Jack, than to learn I'm Keno McQueen."

"Yeah? Well, she'll find out, all right. Why don't you blow out your brains and get it over, Keno? Here's my gun if you want it."

A slow, terrible smile crept across the lips of Grover Wingate. "I've contemplated doing just that, my friend. When Jill is safe, and back home again, I may do that little thing. But before I blow my own brains out, Jack, I'm going to make certain that both you and Jack Frost are so dead that you can't ruin that girl's life with proof of her father's black record. She's clean, as clean as God's fresh air and sunshine. She's as good as I am bad. I'll willingly kill any man that tells Jill that her father is Keno McQueen.

"I told you that this would be my last trip across the border. I'm all washed up with the game. I've made mine and I'm stepping out before some fly cop slips me a pair of nice steel bracelets. I've never done time in the Big House. I never will. And if it'll keep my baby girl from busting her heart, pal, I'll snuff out my own candle. But before I do, I'll see her a long way out of reach of your filthy paws. She'll be married to a real man that'll take care of such jackals as you and Jack Frost." Wingate lit a cigar.

From a deck of cards, Jack Liggett flipped three cards. He smiled across the table at his companion. "Two jacks, McQueen," he said, "and the joker. Two knaves, both black ones. Keno McQueen's two jacks . . . Jack Liggett, the knave of spades, and Jack Frost, the knave of clubs." He laid them, one on each side of the joker. "Two knaves, both black. But, McQueen, there's more black on the joker than there is on the two knaves. Sometime when you're in one of these sanctimonious moods, ponder on that."

Jack Liggett tossed off another drink and swaggered out. Keno McQueen was alone. He sat there for a long time, staring at the three cards. He picked up the knave of clubs and tore it into bits. The knave of spades followed. Then he picked up the joker and carefully, painstakingly set it afire with his cigar lighter, and watched it burn to a white ash.

CHAPTER
ELEVEN

Dave pulled the foam-flecked black horse down to a steady road gait. War Bonnet, wet with sweat and sullenly defiant, ate up the miles at a long-legged pace. Easily the best road horse that wore the Seven-Up iron, the black animal's sole handicap was lack of hardness under a saddle. Gentle enough now, but nervous and jumpy when its rider moved abruptly, War Bonnet's hardest lesson was over. Dave talked to the black horse in a low voice as he patted the sweaty neck.

Presently he caught up with Jill Wingate. Her mount was a chestnut sorrel of steel-dust breeding, fast, and as tough as rawhide.

"You and War Bonnet both look like you'd had a bad hour," she said. "I can't help but feel sorrier for the horse than for the man. It must be a terrible thing to be so completely conquered in spirit, so beaten, so licked."

"I'm hoping, Miss Wingate," replied Dave, wiping the dust and blood and perspiration from his face in an effort to appear less obnoxious, "to make War Bonnet savvy that I'm his pardner, not his owner. I'd bet a hat that after this pony meets Biscuits and Dynamite and they have a powwow with him, he'll look at me more friendly."

"Biscuits and Dynamite?"

"My private horse and pack mule. They do everything but talk. And there was a time when Biscuits was an outlaw like War Bonnet. As for Dynamite, he'd kick anyone that came near him. His Mexican owner swapped him to me for a quart of tequila." Unbuckling his field glasses, he passed them to the girl. "That dust cloud behind me has been getting me thinking, ma'am. Will you see what's kicking it up?"

They halted and the girl focused the glasses. "Some men on horseback."

"I thought so. Now, if War Bonnet will stand still about a minute, I'll take a look."

Dave picked up the riders. Five of them. Their gun barrels glittered in the sunlight. They were coming at a fast clip.

"Something's gone wrong," Dave told her as he put away the glasses. "Those five gents aren't riding for pleasure this morning. There's a dark boy in Jack Liggett's woodpile, ma'am. I reckon we better let our ponies out another notch. We're an hour from the border. Your horse is fresh and stout. War Bonnet will make it, if I don't crowd him too hard. Once we reach the line, we're safe enough. I have a couple of friends on duty there. Once across the border, I can outfox 'em."

"I warned you," said Jill Wingate, "that you overplayed your hand when you told Jack Liggett about being wanted by the Immigration officers."

"Yeah?" Dave grinned at her with lips that were swollen from Cutter's punishing hands. "I reckon, lady, that you didn't see so good with these glasses. There's two Immigration men leading that gang. It looks to me like they meant it. Dent, Taller, and the Goldie gent complete the posse. Something's gone wrong." Dave sent her a quick look of suspicion. "Directly we get across the line, we'll pull up and kind of comb the kinks outta this proposition. Let's go!"

Carefully, with the skill of a man who understands horseflesh, Dave jockeyed the half-broken War Bonnet along the trail. He wanted to get all speed possible out of the black horse without breaking the animal's spirit. And as he rode, he tried to piece together the stories of Jill Wingate and Jack Liggett and arrive at a somewhat truthful solution. He knew that the girl had evaded the truth somehow. He had been quick to sense the falsity of Jack Liggett's proposition. He wondered if they had led him into a trap, using this girl as bait. Such things had been done. Wiser men than Dave had been caught like that. And he was dealing with the cleverest smuggling ring on the border.

The five men were gaining. But they were still a long distance behind when Dave and the girl reached a board shack that was a sentry station of the Border Patrol.

Two Customs men stepped out of the shack. Two Mexican officials popped out, bristling with guns. Dave and the girl halted.

"¡Buenos días, señores!" called Dave. The Mexicans grinned a welcome. The two Americans were staring hard at Dave, as if they could not believe what their eyes told them. "Long time no see, boys," said Dave easily to them.

"Gosh, Captain," spoke one of them, "you sure gave me a start. I knew those boneheads would turn you loose. What's up?"

"Same old racket, boys. That's why I worked it so you two boys would be transferred here. There'll be no slip this time." Dave jerked a thumb back over his shoulder. "When those birds get here, stop 'em. Two of 'em are Immigration boys that are all in a sweat about something. The other three are Jack Liggett's men. Can you keep 'em from coming across the line?"

"If you say so, Captain, we sure can," said the taller of the two Customs officers. "You got me this job when I left the cavalry, Captain. I saw 'em railroad you. Right or wrong, I'm for you. Stop those guys? I'll tell a rookie."

"I don't know what kind of a line they'll hand you, boys. It looks like some jasper has pitched a monkey wrench into my works. So they may tell you I'm kidnapping Miss Wingate or that I'm wanted for murder or something else. *¿Quién sabe?* When I gave my guards the slip somewhere in Kansas, I left there in a rush. I've traveled far and fast since then. And I haven't taken the Immigration Service into my confidence. But you boys were with me in France, so I reckon I don't need to go into details. Act dumb, see? You know the old game. If that Lowry gent wants to cross very bad, let him come. But hold those cowpunchers. They're McQueen's men. And if I get a decent break this time, I'm throwing the hooks into our old *compadre*, Keno McQueen. Miss Wingate is helping me. Something big is about to pop. Watch this border close. Nab anybody that crosses north, regardless of passport. The time fuse on this bomb is set for about ten days from now, but it may go off prematurely. When it busts, it's gonna blow up McQueen and his pack."

Dave turned to the Mexicans. In their own language he asked them the location of Colonel Herrera's camp. They gave it with ready tongue, for they were of Herrera's little band of hard-riding constabulary.

"And did Colonel Herrera leave my horse here?"

"At the corral in the arroyo, *señor*."

"'*Sta bueno*." Dave squinted at the fast-approaching dust cloud. "I reckon, ma'am, that it's time we moved along. Remember, boys, act dumb."

Dave and Jill Wingate rode on. She kept looking at him with a disconcerting scrutiny. Dave led the way down a deep arroyo to a large corral where a dozen horses and mules were eating hay.

Dave turned War Bonnet into the corral and threw his saddle on Biscuits. Both Biscuits and Dynamite were given a biscuit apiece from Dave's pocket. The girl looked on in amused silence.

Again they rode on, side-by-side, at a stiff gait. Now and then Dave looked back along the trail. Presently he halted, pointing back.

"Our persistent friend, the Immigration man," he said. "Will you give me your word not to run away if I leave you here? Or had I better tie you up to a mesquite tree?"

"Why should I run away," she asked, "unless you are playing a crooked game and plan on using me as a pawn? I came with you willingly. You have promised to save my father. Should I cease to trust you?"

"So long as you are square with me, Miss Wingate, I'll shoot square with you. When I've taken care of this Lowry gent, I'll come back. We'll have some lunch and a talk that'll do us both plenty of good. I'd trust you, even against my own fears. *¡Adiós!*" And turning his horse, he galloped back to meet the approaching horseman. She watched him with misty eyes.

"If only I could trust you, Captain Higgins," she said huskily, and, touching her restive horse with her spurs, she swung off the trail and headed for the broken rim of the three craters where, unknown to her, Jack Frost and three other men were camped, waiting for the coming of Keno McQueen and Jack Liggett. For more than a mile Jill Wingate rode at a furious pace. Tears filled her eyes and she choked back the sobs that rose in her throat. Then she pulled up and with an angry gesture, wiping the tears from her eyes. "I'll trust you, Dave Higgins, even against my own fears," she said, and with her head tilted gallantly upward, she rode slowly back toward the spot where Dave would expect to find her if she held true to their bond of trust.

CHAPTER
TWELVE

Tex Lowry rode with drawn gun toward Dave, who sat his motionless horse with upraised hands.

"Well, Lowry?"

"I want you, Higgins." Lowry's tone was brittle, his eyes hard slits of dangerous light.

"So it seems, old trooper." Dave grinned. "But I hope to gosh you haven't tipped my name to Liggett and those men of his."

"Liggett's out of this. This lies between you and me. Where did you get that ring you're wearing? I want the truth."

"You knew the boy that owned this ring, Lowry? You knew R.L.?"

"Bob Lowry is my kid brother, Higgins. How did you get his ring?"

"Let's get off our horses, Lowry," said Dave gently, "and I'll tell you what I know. The boy is dead, old man. He was shot in the back, without a chance. Easy, man. I wouldn't be telling you this if I had a hand in his murder." Dave looked unflinchingly into the muzzle of Tex Lowry's gun.

Lowry lowered the weapon and the two men got off their horses. And as gently as he could, Dave told him of the death of the boy down along *El Camino de Chinos*. When Dave finished talking, a hush fell over the two men. Something of the brightness of the morning had dulled. Dave took off the ring and handed it to Lowry.

"Why did they let a boy like that go alone into this country?" asked Dave. "Even an old-timer at this game runs big chances of not getting out alive, once he's seen *El Camino de Chinos*. What's the government thinking of?"

"Bob was no longer in the service, Higgins. He'd been kicked out, disgraced. One of McQueen's snakes had planted a package of dope in the kid's car. They framed him. And a blind fool jury would have sent him to the pen. Bob broke jail and came down here to clear his name. They got him, as I knew they'd get him, Higgins."

Dave nodded, rolling a cigarette into shape. "So you found me at Liggett's place and sized me up as being one of McQueen's men, eh? It never occurred to you that McQueen smashed me as he smashed your young brother, that I was down here to clear the name of Captain Dave Higgins. No, you wouldn't think of that. I hope you didn't tell Liggett that you recognized me?"

"That's just what I did, when you gave me the slip. I reckon I lost my head for a minute. The sight of this ring of Bob's upset me."

"Liggett knows I'm Dave Higgins, then?"

"Yes. Liggett is in with McQueen?"

"He is. Jack Liggett is McQueen's right bower."

"And where is McQueen?"

115

"I don't know where he is now, Lowry, but I know where I'll put him, once I get his number. Unless he outfigures me. Your only play now," Dave went on grimly, "is to trot on back to the Seven-Up Ranch. Tell Liggett I gave you the slip down here. Then pull out with your partner. Lay low. Keep an eye on the ranch. If Jack Liggett tries to rabbit, nab him. But don't keep him from crossing into Mexico. He and McQueen have a big plant down here somewhere. No, not Chinamen. More likely it's dope. They plan on coming after it and taking it back. I have men planted down here watching Jack Frost and three more men who are riding herd on this plant. Keep in contact with the two Customs men at the shack. Be ready to snap the pinchers on Liggett if I give the word from down here. They'll work fast, now that they know I'm down here. I was closer than this before, Lowry, when they outfoxed me and smashed me. The rumor may come out that I'm dead. You may even see my dead body. But when the word reaches you from down here, nab Liggett dead or alive."

"How about McQueen?"

"Can't tell about him till we spot him. He may be just a myth, but I think not. He may be one of Liggett's guests. Or he may be a woman."

"I never thought of that. The Wingate woman?"

"I haven't made an opinion, Lowry. I'm just guessing. But get Liggett."

"How about Jack Frost?"

"Jack Frost," said Dave flatly, "will be dead."

"I'd like the job of killing him, if he killed Bob," said Lowry heavily.

116

"That's my job, Lowry, by prior claim. An old debt, savvy?"

"I'm sorry, Higgins, that I gummed up the cards here."

"No use worrying over it. It'll have the effect of hastening their next move, and for that I'm thankful. By the way, Lowry, you'll learn in a day or so that I've kidnaped Wingate's daughter. So don't let that bit of news get you off on a tangent."

Lowry whistled noiselessly. "Gosh, man! Grover Wingate's worth millions! He'll have you hung to the first tree in sight. You're not serious?"

"But I am. Fact is, the lady herself got me the job. Liggett hired me. And a friend of mine tipped me off that her father is also in on it. Figure it out for yourself."

"It's a trap."

"Mebby so," said Dave, dropping back into the range vernacular as easily as a man changing hats. "On the other hand, mebby not. But it's a game worth playing, even if I lose. Well, I'll be drifting along. Keep your mouth shut and your eyes open. See you someday soon."

And Dave rode back to where Jill Wingate sat her horse, awaiting his return. Their glances met and parried like the rapiers of two skilled fencers. Then Dave laughed softly.

"You seem amused," she said. "Perhaps your friend, Lowry, passed along some joke? Frankly I see nothing humorous in the situation."

117

"Even in Mexico, lady," said Dave gravely, "they let a man laugh at his own execution. Friend Lowry tells me that I'm due to hang or be shot before long. Jack Liggett and Company have found out my identity. I happen to be the little knot in their otherwise smooth-running rope. Their combine broke me once, ma'am, smashed me, disgraced my name, and sent me to federal prison. Liggett never saw me before. They have hired help that attends to such cases as mine was. I was in their way. They simply eliminated me, as one might solve a not too difficult problem in mathematics. I got free somehow. I came back, Miss Wingate, to break up a dangerous ring of crooks."

"I suspected as much when I first saw you." The girl nodded. "I'd heard of the case of Captain Wallace David Higgins. I'd seen a picture of you in an El Paso paper. I was there during your trial and the papers were full of the scandal. Today, when the two Customs men called you captain, that picture clicked into place. You are a brave man, Captain Higgins, as well as a fool. You're outnumbered and you're playing the game on their field. You haven't a chance."

"Mexico, Miss Wingate, is any man's ground, so long as he's forking a fast horse and has a belt full of cartridges." Dave patted the neck of the buckskin horse and smiled at her. "Miss Wingate," he said, looking at her with troubled eyes, "I'd like better than anything I can name to be able to trust you. I want to help you. You're in trouble, such grave trouble that you have lied to me and even now you're risking your honor and life by coming down here. You're doing this for your father.

You tell me one story. Liggett wastes half an hour with another elaborate lie. The whole thing has the earmarks of a well-laid trap. Yet I'm fool enough to believe in you and want to help you. But I can't be of much assistance unless you tell me the truth."

"My father's life is in great danger," she said in a lifeless tone. "If it becomes necessary, I'll sacrifice my life, and yours, also, to save him. That Lowry has spoiled my plan." She pulled up her horse. "I'd better turn back here, Captain Higgins. I give you my word of honor not to tell Jack Liggett anything I've learned. I wish you luck. May God guide you safely out of this country of death. Good bye."

"Sorry, Miss Wingate, but you're not going back to the ranch." Dave reached over and grabbed her bridle rein. His face was set in grim lines.

With a quick move, the girl's heavy quirt slashed him across the face. But he still held the rein and his face showed white save for the angry red welt. Biscuits swung alongside the girl's horse. Dave's arms went around her. The struggle was furious, brief, one-sided. Dave threw the quirt away and pocketed the automatic that he wrenched from her hand. Then he rode on, leading her horse, without a backward glance at the white-lipped, panting girl who sat her saddle with futile anger.

For more than an hour, they rode like that in silence. Dave took out the map given him by Liggett, studied it with narrowed eyes, and handed it to the girl with a faint smile.

"Nice map, ma'am. Reminds me of a spider showing the fly how to get into the center of the web. You see, I've just returned from a little scouting trip down here. I happen to know that Jack Frost and three other McQueen men are waiting at the spot where I'm supposed to keep you a prisoner. Liggett overplayed his hand. He's too elaborate. And so he used you to trap me, eh? It might have worked, too, if I wasn't familiar with this country down here. He expects to play me into Jack Frost's hands, eh? Well, that's Jake with me. I'll do just that. But not today or perhaps not tomorrow. We'll just pull off the trail and make camp. And when McQueen and Jack Liggett ride down to the craters to meet Jack Frost, I'll lope over that way and bag the whole gang."

Dave saw the girl go white. She bit her lip in a desperate fight for self-control.

"Jack Liggett, Frost, and the elusive Keno McQueen will be caught in their own trap. My men have orders to shoot to kill." Dave saw her grip the saddle horn as she fought against faintness. He felt cowardly and despicable as she looked at him with the eyes of a beaten child.

"You win, Captain Higgins," she said in a husky whisper. She handed back the map with a little shudder. "I don't ask you to believe me, but I swear by the soul of my dead mother that I did not know we rode to meet Jack Frost. It's just another of Jack Liggett's devilish ideas of torture. Liggett hates me. He's afraid of me. And because I'd rather be dead than to have Jack Frost touch me, he takes this means of

120

punishing me. When I said my father's life was in danger, I did not lie. I spoke no word last night that I did not believe with all my heart. It was only after I returned to the ranch, after Cutter was killed, that I learned the truth. I learned that my father knew I was to be taken here and kept prisoner. That I would be safely returned was understood from the start. But I was to be hidden away until Keno McQueen and Jack Liggett came down here and returned again to the ranch. I had learned something of their traffic in contraband, enough to be dangerous to their plans. So I was to be hidden away until the stuff was taken across the border and disposed of. Liggett gave me my choice of that or death to my father. Because you looked decent, I chose you in preference to Sonora Dent or Goldie or Taller. Because Liggett suspected you for a spy, and because he is ready to strike at my father and me, he has drawn this map that was intended to send you to your death and to send me into worse than death. Jack Liggett has broken his promise to me. He's burning his bridges. He knows that this is his last haul and he's planning to make a getaway. When he leaves the Seven-Up Ranch, he quits it forever. He'll never voluntarily go back across the border. He'll board a yacht at Skeleton Bay."

Jill Wingate was approaching a state of hysteria. Dave tried his best to follow her thoughts. But he was unprepared for her next statement.

"I swear to you, Captain Higgins, that until I accidentally overheard a conversation between Father and Liggett last night, I did not know that Grover Wingate was Keno McQueen."

Her voice had thinned to a shrill whisper. Dave caught her as she toppled sideways from her saddle.

CHAPTER
THIRTEEN

Dave still held the girl in his arms when he reached the water holes two miles away. She was conscious now, moaning a little as she clung to him. Though no words passed her lips, her eyes begged him for mercy — mercy for her father who was a criminal, a man who had sent other men to death or to prison for crimes they had never committed.

He had lit a fire and was broiling a rabbit he had shot when Colonel Estaban Herrera rode up with a prisoner. The prisoner was Spud Shanley.

"Say," sputtered the little prizefighter, "tell dis boid to toin me loose, champ."

"Spud's all right, Steve." Dave grinned. "I thought you'd be coming along this way, both of you."

"Son-of-a-gun, how this small one fight," said the Mexican. "He rides to meet the *Señor* Jack Frost, no?"

"Got a note for Frost, Spud?" asked Dave, as he loosened the ropes that held Spud trussed in his saddle.

Spud passed over a note written in code. Dave, in return, gave him the little tin box that he had again found in its hiding place under the rimrock. The box held the messenger's ration of cocaine, which Spud brazenly put to use.

123

Dave led Colonel Herrera over to where Jill sat in an attitude of listless defeat, and introduced the suave and gallant Mexican.

"Circumstances have been unkind in literally throwing Miss Wingate into our midst, Steve. Can you possibly make her comfortable at your camp?"

With voluble tongue, the gallant colonel assured the girl that she would be well taken care of. His camp was but a short distance. There she would find every comfort possible in such a thrice-cursed and god-forgotten strip of miserable land. His earnest assurances brought a smile to the girl's lips. He apologized for his appearance, his very existence, for the heat and the lack of water, for the sparsity of shade. His fervor had Dave chuckling. Jill joined in the laughter that followed Herrera's condemnation of his native land.

"Miss Wingate will be returning to the Seven-Up Ranch in the morning," said Dave. "Spud will act as her escort, and perhaps you can give them an escort of two or three men."

"A dozen men," came the gallant offer.

"You mean I'm free to go back?" asked the girl when the colonel and Spud were tending to their horses.

"Tomorrow." Dave nodded as he decoded the note to Jack Frost from Jack Liggett.

"And the conditions, Captain Higgins?"

"We'll speak of them later, when you've been made more comfortable."

"There are conditions, then?" Jill Wingate's tone was a little scornful.

Dave looked up from his decoding task with a faint smile. "I'm giving Keno McQueen his life and liberty. In return for that, I ask as much from him and from you. I ask for my chance to wipe the black stain from my name and honor as an Army officer."

"You won't harm my father?" she asked.

"Your father is only a name behind which Jack Frost and Jack Liggett have hidden. His position, as near as I've learned, is that of a fence, or clearing-house, for the smuggled contraband. They've quietly spread the name Keno McQueen as a menace to lesser smugglers. Frost and Liggett have done the actual killing and other dirty work. I doubt if Grover Wingate gets a dollar from the smuggled proceeds."

"You really believe that?" She had taken one of Dave's hands in both of hers, clinging desperately to it as a drowning person hangs to a bit of driftwood.

"If I didn't know that to be true, I'd keep you here and let Keno McQueen walk into my trap. That, despite the fact that I've fallen hopelessly in love with his daughter. Did you know that I loved you, Jill?"

"No, I did not know."

Herrera and Spud were returning. Dave, still gripping her two hands, looked into her gray eyes, eyes that were no longer dulled with bitter pain. "Tonight, at camp, you'll let me tell you about it, Jill?"

"Yes. Yes, Dave. Tonight."

And so that night, under the starlit Mexican sky, Dave forgot danger, and, shutting his eyes to that which he did not wish to envisage, he told Jill Wingate, daughter

125

of a crook, that he loved her and would always love her, that he would endure anything in the world except the loss of her, if she loved him.

And Jill Wingate, remembering that her father was Keno McQueen, wondered why God had been so kind in sending her the love of this man, and why fate was so relentlessly cruel as to snatch away that love again.

"For our love is so impossible, Dave," she whispered as he held her close in his arms. "You can't face your world with a wife whose father is a notorious crook."

"You love me, Jill?"

"Yes, Dave. With every bit of my heart and soul."

"Then," Dave told her with a grim sort of elation, "that settles it. There are other countries . . . Mexico, for instance, South America. No one will know or care who we are so long as I make good at my job. I have a little money. I know the cow business. I love you as I'll never love another woman. I wouldn't swap your love for a dozen Army careers. I'd planned on quitting the Army, anyhow, as soon as I'd cleared my name. With War Bonnet, Biscuits, and Dynamite, we'll be mounted, anyhow. I have friends in Mexico. Steve Herrera, for instance. Land is cheap. I have enough to buy a few cows and lease a ranch. Why, Jill, we're lucky."

And so he forgot his tomorrows in the dreams of tonight. And that is the magic way of men in love.

In the early dawn, Jill Wingate and Spud, with an escort of troopers, set out for the Seven-Up Ranch. Jill was taking a message to her father. Spud carried a coded message from Jack Frost to Jack Liggett, while both Spud and the girl carried back with them a simple story of the death of Dave Sandborne, cowboy. He had been killed by a roving band of Indians. Jill had been rescued by Spud and these brave Mexican troopers, who were likewise coached to tell the same tale.

Dave himself had sent the message to Jack Liggett, so wording it that the note sounded like Frost. The message, that now was in the tin box under the rimrock waiting for Frost, was also of Dave's composition. The real messages were in Dave's billfold.

The trap was set. Each actor in this bit of life's drama had been carefully coached in his part. As the sun crept like a huge ball of red fire up over the broken skyline, Dave and Estaban Herrera smiled grimly into each other's eyes.

To the south, where white whalebones dotted the smooth sand of Skeleton Bay, a yacht rode at anchor. White, trim, graceful, it waited the coming of Jack Liggett, its master. And, hidden in the dunes, two of Estaban Herrera's men watched it, day and night.

"Now," said Dave, pinching out the coal of his cigarette, "all we need do is leave *El Camino de Chinos* open and let Liggett and the wily Jack Frost ride along it for the last time. They're planning to meet at the water holes. I've changed the hour of their meeting to midnight tonight. Only with this slight variation. In the note to Jack Frost, I put the time at eleven o'clock, sharp. In the note to Liggett, I made the hour exactly midnight. Liggett will get there second, savvy?

127

McQueen will be with him, I think. Liggett and Frost plan to kill McQueen and Frost's three companions there at the water holes."

"Eh?" Herrera smiled incredulously. He had no knowledge that Jill Wingate's father was Keno McQueen. Dave took out the decoded notes. "Kill Keno McQueen? Impossible!" Herrera's hands went out in an expressive gesture.

"Listen to this note written by Jack Frost to Jack Liggett."

Meet me at water holes. Three fences getting spooky as hell. Up to us to feed them three pills of hot lead. Two of Captain Higgins's men on duty at border. Lowry is R.L.'s brother. Looks like tight border. That means back-trail to yacht and clear for keeps. Have million in actual value this haul. Will make New York entry with stuff. Only bet now. No see blue-eyed man buckskin horse, but got tip Higgins is loose. Looks like something gone wrong.

Dave grinned at the Mexican. "That's that, Steve. Our friend Jack Frost smells a rat. They use the yacht as a back-door getaway. Clever, too. And Frost suggests a New York entry with the contraband. Now listen to what McQueen and Liggett sent out in the way of love letters." Dave took another code note from his wallet.

Higgins headed your way. Get him. Jill with him. Send her back to ranch. Will meet you at water holes in two days. Be there with stuff and three fences. Must use boat this time. Things haywire here. Get Higgins.

"That," said Dave, "was evidently written in McQueen's presence. Listen to this second one that Liggett slipped Spud when McQueen wasn't looking."

Higgins and girl headed for your camp. Kill him and do as you please about girl. As I always suspected, Keno is crossing us. I think he knew Higgins was out. I'm dead sure he recognized H. at the ranch and let him take Jill away. He figures H. has us in the sack, and he wants us caught. He'll bump himself off if cornered, once the girl is safe. So when we meet at water holes I'll have McQueen with me. Get him and I'll give you the girl with my blessing, though a woman on a boat is bad luck. This place is getting unhealthy. Argentine good market for our wares. Get Higgins. We might as well leave three fences with McQ. at the water holes. And if you have half a brain, kill the girl or send her back here.

"And so," said Dave, as he put away the code messages, "we sent the girl back, but not with Jack Frost's permission. She and Spud have a straight story that can't be broken by cross-examination. I've sent McQueen word to come along with Liggett, but to watch for tricks. So tonight I'll meet Frost at eleven o'clock. And when Liggett gets to the water holes at midnight, he'll meet me instead of Jack Frost."

"And the *Señor* McQueen?" asked Herrera.

"McQueen goes back with me, to stand trial. His real name is Wingate, Steve. The girl is his daughter. Wingate is more fool than he is crook. As I figure it, he's their market for the contraband stuff. As receiver of stolen or smuggled property, he's due to cool his heels in prison. The name McQueen is just a bogey-man name to scare the little fellows in the smuggling game. McQueen's sick of the game, but doesn't dare withdraw. But he'd give his very life to see Liggett and Frost put out of business. There's the whole idea, savvy? As for these three men referred to as fences, they are the men selling the contraband to Liggett and Frost. Chinamen, maybe, probably scared stiff by now, poor devils."

"Do not forget this, Dave," warned Estaban Herrera. "It is the man who is scared stiff who sometimes fights like hell. Because one cannot figure the moves of a coward, he can be damned dangerous. So, we'll have to watch those fences."

"You and I, Steve, will wait for those men at the water holes. They'll have the contraband with them. Send a detail of men to Skeleton Bay to cover that retreat. Get a messenger to the boys at the border to grab off Sonora Dent, Taller, and Goldie quietly and without upsetting the guests at the ranch, after McQueen and Liggett pull out."

"Perhaps those three will come along with McQueen and Liggett?" suggested the Mexican.

"In that case," replied Dave, "you and I will have our hands full."

"Dave," said Estaban Herrera smiling, "you may be certain of that."

CHAPTER
FOURTEEN

By the luminous hands of Colonel Estaban Herrera's wrist watch it was 11:00p.m. White moonlight bathed the rough hills with a ghostly, shadowy glow. Four men rode single file along the trail to the water holes, their horses dropping off the slope into the arroyo. On the opposite side of the arroyo squatted Dave, a carbine in his hands, his eyes following the four riders. He wondered where their pack animals were, for a fortune in drugs would be rather bulky.

The man who rode in the lead wore a high-crowned white Stetson but was otherwise in nondescript rags. Dave's pulse quickened as he watched that white hat sway with the motion of the horse. He was sure it was Jack Frost, the killer, handsome, dangerous, treacherous, stepson of Bill Higgins and so half-brother of the man who now crouched in the shadow, Winchester in his hands. Dave fought back a sensation akin to nausea. From the opposite side of the narrow arroyo Estaban Herrera watched, a flickering smile on his tight lips, a cocked gun ready. For the Mexican knew that Dave would give his blackguard half-brother a fighting chance, and that the treacherous Jack Frost would kill him.

Dave concentrated his attention on the white hat. He depended on his Mexican partner to attend to the other three. Gripping his gun, Dave stood up.

"Halt where you are!" He barked the command in a harsh voice.

"*¡Carramba!*" grunted Estaban, and fired without further delay. The last man of the four riders fell from his saddle, grazed by the Mexican's bullet, his gun spitting staccato flame even as he fell.

The white-hatted rider cut loose with an automatic. Dave's first shot smashed his shoulder.

"Yoy, meester, don't shoot!" came a cry as the four frightened horses milled in confusion.

But the fallen man who lay on the ground kept shooting. "Fight, fools!" he snarled up at them. "Fight, you gutless rats!"

"*Kamerad!*" bellowed the man in the white hat. "I'm shot! *Gott in Himmel!*"

Estaban Herrera, with a swift leap, was on top of the cursing man on the ground, who had only stopped shooting because his gun was empty.

Dave, realizing his mistake, scrambled down the rocks and set about jerking the three men from their horses, starting with the wounded one in the white hat.

Herrera and the disguised Jack Frost were locked in deadly embrace. For a few brief moments they fought. Two knives flashed. Then the Mexican rose to his feet, his long knife red to the hilt. Jack Frost, in his nondescript rags of disguise, lay very still, a slowly widening stream of red staining his breast and throat.

133

Dave was herding his three prisoners, who babbled in a jargon of mixed German and Yiddish, except for the wounded man waving their arms in terrified gestures.

"The *Señor* Jack Frost," stated Estaban Herrera as he stepped across the motionless body, "will shoot no more men in the back. I recognized that foxy one as he rode down the trail."

"You hurt, Steve?" asked Dave.

"*Pouff!* A small scratch on the face. Another on the . . . *Santa Maria*, look!" He pointed up the trail.

Two horsemen were coming at breakneck speed out of the night.

"Quick, Steve, lend a hand with this rope," breathed Dave. In panting haste they bound the three scared-faced, babbling prisoners, then shoved rude gags into their mouths. They had no sooner completed their task than the two riders dropped at a run off the slope and into the arroyo.

"Stick 'em up, you two!" snapped Dave.

"Wait!" called the unmistakable voice of Spud Shanley. "Hold everyt'ing, champ!"

"Don't shoot, Higgins! It's Wingate!" called Spud's companion.

"Good gosh," growled Dave. "Where's Liggett?"

"Coming," gasped Wingate, swaying as he held to his saddle horn. "He's just behind us. He and Dent and Taller and Goldie. Liggett got hold of the note you sent me . . . he was torturing Spud when I found him . . ."

"Dis Dent boid had a hunch, see, dat it was me as done fer Cutter. Dey was giving me de t'oity-t'oid degree when de guvnor here busts into de game with a gat. Den hell busts loose. De guvnor's bad hoit, champ. Slip him a drink."

"Never mind me." Wingate got off his horse and sat down. "I've lost a little blood, that's all. Better get set for those men that are coming, Higgins."

"Where's Jill?" asked Dave.

"Safe at the Customs station, thank God. She wanted to come, but that was out of the question. Where's Frost?"

"Jack Frost is dead." Dave bent over the ugly hole in Wingate's thigh, wrapping a crude bandage and tourniquet about the leg.

"Good. Watch these three men you have, Higgins. And stake me to a weapon of some sort. I'm a miserable shot, but . . . there they come."

A spattering hail of rifle fire came from the mesa.

Dave turned to Herrera. "Take charge, will you, Steve?"

"*¡Si!* You think the *Señor* Liggett will run for it?"

"Exactly. He'll coyote on us, sure as hell. And I want him. Let Wingate guard the three prisoners. You and Spud pick off Dent and his two men. I'll catch Liggett at Skeleton Bay."

Dave scrambled up the bank and crawled into some brush to where his buckskin horse was tied.

"Let's go, Biscuits!"

Dave had discarded his Winchester for the more wieldy Colt six-shooter. He sat his saddle, holding back his restive horse as he peered into the night. Then he gave Biscuits a free rein, lay low across the horse's neck, and tore at a run into the open.

A rifle spewed flame from a brush patch, but the man's aim was hasty. Biscuits twisted in dodging leaps along the crooked trail. The brush hid horse and rider now as they raced along the trail that led to Skeleton Bay.

Intuition told Dave that somewhere ahead of him rode Jack Liggett. For the wily smuggler knew that the Customs men would be in hot pursuit. Lowry and Sam would be on his trail. And there were the Mexican border riders to contend with. Jack Liggett would ride as fast as horseflesh could carry him toward the safety of that yacht that lay at anchor. He was heading for the back door of *El Camino de Chinos*.

CHAPTER
FIFTEEN

Dave, pushing Biscuits hard, heard the sound of rifle fire when he was still some distance from Skeleton Bay. *That,* figured Dave, *will be Herrera's men and Liggett. And Liggett's boat crew, perhaps, lending their boss a hand.*

As he rode at a long lope for the rolling sand dunes, he saw the flash of guns and heard shouts, confused commands. Above the scattered rifle fire came another sound, a sound that sent a quick shiver along Dave's spine. There was no mistaking the rat-tat-tat-tat of machine-gun fire.

Then half a dozen horsemen raced from the dunes in headlong flight. For the Mexicans, lacking the leadership of the daring and war-tried Colonel Herrera and badly disconcerted by the rattle of the machine-gun, were making a hasty and none too orderly retreat.

"*¿Quién es?*" barked Dave as they came at a run toward him. "Hi! Hi! *!Caballeros!*"

A sergeant in charge babbled a panicky explanation. "A hundred of the *gringo* devils, *señor!* A dozen machine-guns! *¡Madre de Dios!*"

"Then, *hombres,*" cried Dave, "I will show you that one brave man can make those same *gringos* scatter like

137

rabbits! Where have they placed that machine-gun?" Dave felt none of the confidence that he pretended. He saw, in his mind's eye, Jack Liggett sailing safely away, thumbing a derisive gesture from the deck of the slim-lined greyhound of the sea. But he wanted these Mexicans to fight once more. "Dismount, *caballeros! ¡Pronto!* Scatter out among the dunes. Keep up a steady fire. I'll take care of the gun crew. Your job is to keep them busy. If a skiff pulls out from shore, concentrate on it. Fill it so full of holes that it will sink. *¿Sabe, hombrecitos?*"

"*Si, señor*," snapped the sergeant, swallowing his fright.

"Make Colonel Estaban Herrera proud of you, then. Go!"

Dave leaped from his horse and ran ahead of them. A moment and he was lost from sight among the dunes. He had jerked a second Colt from a shoulder scabbard, and, with these two weapons, he made his way with all the cunning of an Apache toward the spot from whence came that slithering, clacking hail of machine-gun fire.

A man leaped up in front of him, so close that Dave could see his eyes.

"You, eh, Dent?" he snarled, and fired. Dent wilted, slid to a crumpled heap, and lay still. Dave shoved a fresh shell into his gun before he moved from his crouched position. He expected a shot from Liggett, but none came. Then, zigzagging at a crouching run, he went on.

138

The machine-gun had gone suddenly silent. Dave crept on all fours now. He could hear men cursing with excited fervor.

"The damn' thing's jammed . . . Shell stuck in the magazine . . . gimme a hand here, you . . . now slip me that fresh magazine an' . . . hell!"

Dave's two guns belched into the little knot of men who fussed with the stopped gun.

"At 'em, men!" barked Dave to an imaginary following. "Kill the rats!" Shooting, clubbing, he was in their confused midst. The smell of powder stung his nostrils. He was fighting like a madman, shooting to kill, clubbing at bobbing heads.

Something hot seared his shoulder. A clubbed rifle knocked him off his feet. He felt smothered and confused. Blood and sand and sweaty dungarees. Groans. Curses. He crawled up out of the smothering mass into clean air, shooting at anything that moved.

Both guns empty, Dave stood there, half dazed, the hammers of his guns snapping on empty shells. And he laughed crazily when he saw that he stood alone and that one of the three men sprawled in the sand was crawling toward him with a knife. Dave saw the white face of the fellow, smeared with blood, sneering at him. Then the crawling body pitched forward and the bloody face slid into the sand and did not move again.

Mechanically Dave ejected empty shells from one of his guns. His right arm felt numb and ached with a throbbing pain from neck to fingertips. He pushed fresh shells into the chambers of the single-action .45 that was smeared red with blood and sand.

Then across the sand dunes a horseman rode squarely at him, shooting as he came. Dimly, as in a nightmare, he saw the rider come at him and knew that it was Jack Liggett.

From across the water came the boom of a four-pounder, the clear notes of a bugle, a megaphoned voice: "Heave to and drop your mud hook, or I'll send the pack of you to Davy Jones!"

"I'm crazy," mumbled Dave. "Crazy. Come and get it, Liggett." And he commenced shooting again. Horse and rider were on top of him. Dave went down in a swirl of sand, trying to shoot. His trigger finger was paralyzed. Shod hoofs trampling him into blackness, thundering on, gone, racing for the skiff . . .

Dave tried to crawl to the machine-gun. His limbs were like lead, his arms numb, his head whirling in a red maze of splitting pain. "¡Viva! ¡Viva! Hi! Charge 'em, *caballeros!*" And with fumbling, strengthless hands he groped at the machine-gun. Then he sagged across the gun tripod, his weight sinking the barrel of the gun into the soft sand. And as a black oblivion swallowed him, he heard that mocking voice across the water. "Drop that mudhook, you rats!" *Crazy . . . crazy as hell . . . hearing things . . .*

Dave woke with the splash of cold water in his face. The sun was an hour high. A salty, hearty voice was in his ears; a sub-chaser was at anchor.

"Easy, mate, easy. Lay still. She's been a rough sea. Try a shot of this rum." Dave's eyes saw a weather-reddened, clean-shaven face above the blue uniform of a naval officer, other faces — Estaban Herrera, Wingate, Tex Lowry.

The sting of the liquor felt good. Dave sat up slowly. His left arm was bandaged. His face and head were swathed like a Hindu's turban. There was a gray-haired ship's surgeon washing his hands in a basin filled with pinkish water.

". . . and what I mean, sailor, that cowboy sure put that pepper-box outta commission. Yeah! Kills three guys and shoves the gun in the sand like a ostrich I seen once with his mug shoved . . ."

"Pipe down, Slim. You ain't done nuttin' but pay out tongue since we come ashore. Gimme a hand with this stuff."

Dave, blinking from his bandages, looked about him.

"Feeling better, Captain Higgins?" asked the naval officer.

"Feel like I'd been drunk and woke up in a strange house."

"Take another shot of this rum, then. It'll pick you up. We've made a sweet haul when we bagged that yacht. Got the skipper and what's left of the crew in irons. Liggett, the owner, is dead. Sorry I didn't get him alive. There are some points that need clearing up."

"Liggett is dead?" asked Dave, looking past the officer to Wingate who appeared gray and drawn, as he leaned heavily on a Winchester that was serving as a crutch.

141

"You shot him twice as he rode over you, so Colonel Herrera's men tell me. He toppled off about twenty feet from you."

"Jack Frost is dead," said Dave, holding Wingate's gaze, "and Jack Liggett is dead. There is an old saying that the dead tell no tales." He grinned at the naval officer. "What is it that needs clearing up?"

"This boat is supposed to be a rum-runner and dope-runner. But there's only a few bottles of hooch and no hop at all aboard. We get a hot tip from some chap named Wingate to come to Skeleton Bay and nab Liggett's yacht, the *Gypsy*. We find a small but interesting battle going on and the *Gypsy* getting under way with the skipper and half a crew. And not a thing aboard in the way of contraband. Odd, eh?"

"Perhaps," said Grover Wingate with a wan smile, "I can shed a little light on the subject. The cargo had not been put aboard."

"And who might you be?" scowled the officer.

"I'm Grover Wingate."

"Oh! Your appearance, Mister Wingate, is sort of . . ."

"Villainous." Wingate nodded. "My man, Shanley, will be along in a little bit. He's carrying the stuff. Here he comes now."

Across the dunes came an odd procession. Spud Shanley, mounted on a horse, herding three mules on the backs of which rode three bearded men whose feet were tied under the bellies of their mounts. Behind Spud, who wore an amazing array of cartridge belts looped about his shoulders, rode two Customs men and between the two men rode Jill Wingate.

142

"The cargo of contraband" — Wingate smiled wearily — "is not bulky."

In puzzled silence the men on the shore waited the arrival of Spud and his cavalcade.

CHAPTER
SIXTEEN

Jill Wingate spurred ahead with white lips, fear in her eyes. Flinging herself from her horse, she threw her arms around her father who was smiling through a blur of tears. Then she saw Dave, lying on his sailcloth bed, and, quitting her father with some reassuring whispered words, she kneeled beside Dave.

"I'm all right . . . heaps better than I look." He grinned through the bandages.

"Here's de boids, boss!" Spud told Wingate. "And here's dem belts. Dey wore de hide offen me bones." He dismounted and began shedding cartridge belts. Wingate took one of the cartridges from a belt and began tugging at the bullet.

"Now, sir" — he smiled at the naval officer — "if you'll hold out your cap." And into the cap he shook a bit of cotton and a tiny, glittering object the size of a large pea.

"Diamonds!" gasped the naval officer.

"There is one of these diamonds concealed in each would-be cartridge. Approximately a million dollars worth of stones, all told," said Wingate. He pointed to the three bearded, shifty-eyed prisoners, the one with the wounded shoulder still wore the white hat of the ill-fated Jack Frost. "These three men are known at London headquarters as Red Mike the Pole, who claims that some of these diamonds are part of the Russian crown jewels, Whitechapel Izzy, and Vienna Otto, the three richest and slickest European fences in the game. It's a safe bet that every jewel in the lot is stolen. They don't look so prepossessing just now but in their own shops they are cold-blooded, merciless autocrats. They pay a small sum to the European thieves for the jewels and sell them in Mexico to the men like Frost and Liggett and Keno McQueen, who dispose of the stones at an enormous profit."

"Great Jupiter!" gasped the officer commanding the sub-chaser. "This game makes hop-running look like penny ante. How'd you get wise, Mister Wingate?"

A slow, weary smile spread across Wingate's mouth. Jill stood between her father and Dave, an arm about each of the men she loved. "I am wise to their racket," said Wingate firmly, "because I happen to be Keno McQueen. Captain Higgins is aware of my identity. I made formal surrender to him, some hours ago."

"That's hard to believe, sir," said the naval officer. "You don't look like McQueen, you know."

"But you've never seen Keno McQueen," said the self-condemned crook.

"No. Just heard the name, and, as one will do, conjured up a picture of that master crook. Jove, sir, you must be kidding. You don't look like a criminal."

"Most good crooks look innocent," said Wingate. "That's why it's so hard to catch 'em. Captain Higgins is to be congratulated."

145

"But I say, Wingate or McQueen or whatever you choose to be called, it was you who got word to me to steam down the coast."

"Quite so," agreed Wingate. "I was turning in my fellow crooks. In their parlance, I was squealing. Friend Liggett, being of a suspicious nature, hoped to kill me for my suspected duplicity. He failed. He's dead. So is Frost. Higgins's two Customs men hold two of their men prisoner, Taller and Goldie. When we reach a telegraph station, and I can wire certain police officials, five large diamond merchants will be placed under arrest in San Francisco, Chicago, and New York. I'm coming clean, understand? Wiping my slate. Within twenty-four hours every man connected with this diamond-smuggling ring will be behind the bars." He lit a cigar that was broken and patched with cigarette papers. "All of 'em on the road to prison." Wingate eyed the end of his cigar. "Including the leader, Keno McQueen."

The naval officer eyed Wingate, his daughter, and Dave Higgins. They made an odd picture as they stood there, the brave-eyed girl between the two battered men. Dave broke an uncomfortable silence.

"Will you take charge of the three alien prisoners, sir," he asked the officer, "and the diamonds? I'll be responsible for Mister Wingate."

The officer nodded and saluted stiffly.

"I'll meet you at the Federal Building in San Diego," Dave concluded, "with my prisoners."

And with a heavy heart, Dave turned to where Tex Lowry stood, holding the horses. Estaban Herrera,

146

giving his sergeant a few brief orders to mop up the place, joined Dave as he climbed slowly into his saddle.

"You'll come along, Steve, old buddy?" asked Dave.

"You tell it to the troops, kid, I'm coming, Dave. *Carramba*, what a mess, no? Lowry and I and the amusing Spud shall ride with the *Señor* McQueen. You and the lady come along behind. Snap out from it, old skipper. I, Estaban Herrera, have two good eyes that see what is sticking about to be seen. There is a *padre* at the border. I personally shall attend to the wedding *fiesta*. I shall be what you call the second in your corner. The best *hombre*. I tell you, David, you are a lucky guy. Smile, *compadre!* Snap out from it. *Si*, like that." And the gay Mexican *caballero* got the party under way.

The naval officer bade them an impressive farewell. Estaban, Lowry, and Wingate rode ahead. Spud lingered a moment to talk to Dave, using the adjusting of Jill's saddle blanket as an excuse.

"Say," said the little fellow from the corner of his mouth, "you didn't toin me in, champ. How come?"

"Mum was the word between us two, Spud. You've played square with me and I don't forget things like that. You look shaky, pardner. Need a shot?"

"Like a baby needs milk, kid. But I'm quitting de hop, see? I bin easing off for de last few days. I trou away wot I had. Stringing my bets with a guy like you, pal, has got me thinking, see? I'm quitting de snow for keeps and dat don't mean maybe. You'll need a swipe to look after dese two ponies of your'n, and de mule. I ain't expecting no dough, see? Scoffing and smokes is

147

all I need. Don't let me down, champ." There was pitiful appeal in the eyes under those fist-battered brows of Spud Shanley.

"You won't let him down, will you, Dave?" asked Jill.

"Not in a million years," said Dave.

"Gee," muttered Spud, as Dave gripped his hand. And he rode off before they could see the tears in his eyes.

Oh, Sack O Lee, he killed a man . . .

The words of Spud's tenor-noted melody drifted back across the sand dunes.

"Steve tells me that there's a friend of his at the border, Jill," said Dave, "a *padre* that will marry us."

"You mean you want to marry Keno McQueen's daughter, Dave?" She was smiling as he held her hand. They rode side-by-side, stirrups touching.

"I hope to marry Jill Wingate. I'm not asking for a look at your pedigree, as if I were buying a horse. Will you?"

"Just a minute, Dave," said Jill, withdrawing her hand. "I have something to tell you. It's a message, a very confidential secret. No one but you and me is to share it." She reached into her pocket and took something from it. "Dad gave it to me to give you. You are to give it back to him without a word of comment. Just give it to him when nobody is looking, and say absolutely nothing. Promise?"

"Sure." Dave grinned, wondering at the brightness of her eyes.

148

"And, in return, you'll have to prove yourself. When you promised to serve a certain bold young lady, you listed your accomplishments . . . riding, boxing, roping. Remember? And you claimed you could play a mouth-harp. You've proved it all but the mouth-harp. Have you one?"

For answer, Dave's good hand groped in an overall pocket and pulled forth the mentioned instrument. Jill nodded her approval and held out her hand, closed about some object. Dave pocketed the mouth-harp, his hand covering hers. Something passed from her palm into his. Dave looked at it.

The object was a badge, a gold badge of the U.S. Secret Service. On the back was engraved the name: **Grover Wingate. Colonel, U.S.A.**

Jill smiled through a mist of unshed tears into Dave's astonished face. "Never did I, his own daughter, guess, Dave. And because the government will now put him on another case, we must keep his secret. Put away that badge and play the mouth-harp. Play it loudly. Do you know how to play . . . 'Hail, hail, the gang's all here'?"

"Do I? Listen." And Dave, substituting the mouth-harp for the gold badge, played loudly, so loudly that the riders ahead heard and looked back. Wingate lifted his hat in a gesture that was returned by his daughter.

"Code stuff." Jill smiled. "You may put away the mouth-harp now."

"I get you, honey." Dave grinned. Biscuits and the other horse halted. Dave and Jill were watching the others ride out of sight behind a sand dune.

"I guess I'd better pass this along, Dave. You're to get the Seven-Up Ranch, land, stock, and the good will of the government, for your reward."

"Uh?"

"Thus making safe a strip of the international danger line . . . I think, Dave, that they're out of sight now."

"Gosh!" whispered Dave, and profited, as a soldier should, by valuable information.

The Ranch of the Four Winds

This story under the title "The He-Wolf" by Walt Coburn first appeared in *Action Stories* in the issue dated April, 1928. It was subsequently reprinted by Fiction House under the title "The Ranch of the Four Winds" in *Lariat Story Magazine* in the issue dated June, 1936. The latter had been the author's original title for the story and so it has been retained for its first appearance in book form.

CHAPTER
ONE

A wounded man on a leg-weary horse rode into the dawn that was streaking Desolation Mesa. Ahead of him, magnified in the half light of the new day, bulked a huge stone house, a stone corral, and a long rock barn.

The horseman halted for a moment, his bloodshot eyes fastened on the big stone house. Smoke spiraled into the still air from the huge chimney. The yellow glow of a lamp showed from a window. The man with the wounded thigh drew a .45 Colt and spun the empty cylinder. The loops of his cartridge belt were empty.

Might use the damn' thing for a club, he mused and smiled crookedly, shoving the gun back into the low-tied scabbard on his thigh, the same thigh that oozed sluggish blood through a grimy bandage.

He rode straight for the house. A door opened and a tall, tawny-haired, blue-eyed man stood outlined against the lamplight behind him. The tall man blinked into the dim light and one hand pulled at a drooping yellow mustache. The rider drew rein not five paces from the man in the doorway who stood there motionlessly, without a weapon, a faint smile on his straight mouth.

The man in the saddle swayed a little, as a drunken man accustomed to riding rather than walking might sway. It was as if the long habit of spending endless hours on a horse now kept him in his seat. The face of the swaying rider was gray and haggard, the slit eyes sunken with pain and fatigue.

"I'm looking for Sir John Moss," he croaked in a husky whisper.

"I am John Moss." The tall man in the doorway appeared to ignore the title of knighthood.

"This is the Ranch of the Four Winds, then?"

"Men call my house by that name," said John Moss.

The man in the saddle straightened with an effort that visibly taxed his waning strength. "I came a long way, John Moss, to get to the Ranch of the Four Winds. I fought 'em till I ran outta cartridges. Then me and Black Agate left 'em like they were standing, but they killed my three boys and the missus, and set fire to my place."

The rider's gray face twisted with hate. The man in the doorway now saw that the rider was a man past the sixty mark, a gaunt, gray wolf of a man in a faded hickory shirt and blood-caked overalls. The long, uncut hair under the battered hat was the color of snow. "Who are you, man?" asked John Moss.

"I am the old he-wolf of the Triangle K . . . the man you said needed hanging. I am Barlow Burkett."

As if he had ridden all night to find this rock house and tell its owner this, as if the telling of it sapped his last shred of strength, Barlow Burkett slumped across the neck of the gaunt black horse. John Moss lifted the unconscious man from the saddle and, with an ease that betrayed the superb strength of the muscles under the buckskin shirt, carried the wounded man into the house, the dwelling that was known throughout Arizona as the Ranch of the Four Winds.

An old Indian woman whose face reminded one of a wrinkled, leather mask showed not a trace of any emotion. John Moss addressed her in her own tongue. She brought a surgeon's black kit, hot water, and rolls of bandage into the spare bedroom where John Moss placed the wounded man on a wide bed covered with a sheet. With swift, skilful hands he cut away the unconscious man's clothes. He probed for the bullet with shiny surgical tools.

Old Barlow Burkett's eyes opened, seared red with pain. But he made no outcry as John Moss poked into the raw wound. The leaden slug came out. The wound was bathed and bandaged. Neither man spoke. Then John Moss poured a tumbler half full of raw whiskey and Burkett's powder-blackened hand took the glass.

"Here's thanking you, John Moss." And he gulped down the hot liquor as if it were water. A tinge of color crept into the wounded man's gaunt cheeks. "Lemme know when I'm dying. I've got something to tell you."

"You won't die of that wound, Burkett."

"Thought mebby I'd bled too much. I've seen some good men die from losing too much blood. You wouldn't lie to a man, John Moss?"

"I have no cause to lie," came the quiet reply. "You'll live."

"Then may God have mercy on them as killed my sons and my wife. For I'll kill 'em like I'd kill a nest of snakes."

He lay back on his pillow again, eyes closed under the thick white brows.

"Who attacked your ranch, Burkett?" asked John Moss, washing the blood from his hands in a huge washbowl.

"The Waldrons." Barlow Burkett's eyes were red slits of hate again. "Damn 'em." Then, as the red slits again closed, he added wearily: "You knew that without asking, John Moss."

"Did you get any of them?"

"Cain't say for shore. It was too dark to tell. They took to the brush. They come in the night. Laid a trap. I told Brill he hadn't ought go to the door when the rap came. But they gave our private rap twice and Brill allowed it was a couple of the boys from over on Fossil Crick. They shot him down in his tracks. We'd've made out to hold 'em off but they fired the haystack and the wind was right to catch the house. Those log buildings have been standing for forty years. They caught like shavings. Maw ran out and they shot her. I always kept Black Agate hid in the brush. I think I got Zee Waldron as I rode off. They were shore peppering me. Any of that licker left?"

John Moss gave him another stiff drink. "Better quit talking, Burkett. You've lost a lot of blood."

Barlow Burkett nodded. "One thing I want to ask. Them Waldrons'll be following me. You gonna let 'em kill me when they come?"

"No." John Moss spoke quietly. "Even the wolf is safe in the Ranch of the Four Winds." He walked out, closing the door behind him.

The Indian woman set out breakfast in the long living room. A fire in the huge fireplace took off the chill of the autumn dawn. The firelight threw into relief the giant Briton in his buckskin clothes. He stood with his back to the open fire, hands clasped behind his back, wrapped in deep thought.

For all that he had lived here in the cow country for almost fifteen years, John Moss remained an enigma to everyone. A remittance man with a comfortable quarterly income, he had no need to work for his living. Because he turned no man from his door, friend or enemy, because he was a man of calm judgment, men came here to his house for advice. He settled disputes, gave refuge to hunted men, sat in judgment on land disputes, and in a few cases meted out swift, hard punishment to men who broke faith.

In this land where there was little law of any sort, this stone house became a seat of justice. Within the four rock walls, enemies had shaken hands and were no longer enemies. On one occasion two men had stood facing one another outside in the yard. At a word from John Moss they had emptied their guns at ten paces. Their graves were dug nearby and there those two men were buried. Gentile or Mormon, Indian or white man, outlaw or sheriff stood on equal footing inside the Ranch of the Four Winds. In the little entrance hall was a row of wooden pegs. Here, before they entered the great living room, men unbuckled their guns. On those

157

pegs had hung, side-by-side, the notched guns of an outlaw and the sheriff who wanted him. On another occasion those pegs had held the polished weapons of three Avenging Angels of the Mormon church. Even these three grim-mouthed, bearded men had abode by the word of John Moss. They had carried back word into the Mormon country of a blond giant whose judgment was unbiased. A Mormon bishop, upon hearing their story, sent a letter to John Moss by an Indian. That letter was a message of truce. It was said that John Moss was even permitted to sojourn in those hidden villages where dwelt the polygamous wives of certain Mormons. The Indians called him friend and his eyes had seen their ceremonies.

He had finished breakfast and lit his pipe when a group of horsemen pulled up at the long hitch rack. There were five men in the group, heavily armed, hard-lipped, unsmiling. Three of them bore the name of Waldron. The other two were cowpunchers in their employ. The Waldrons' Flying-W brand was one of the widest-known irons in the entire Southwest. The Waldron clan was comprised of Texans from the *Llanos Estacados* — the Staked Plains. Barlow Burkett also called the *Llanos Estacados* his home.

That strip of Texas cow land was also the birthplace of the terrible range feud between the Burketts and the Waldrons. Like tumbleweeds before a norther, that feud had spread. Blood of both factions spattered the rolling plains. Brothers and uncles and cousins picked the hot-barreled guns from the hands of dead men and vowed to kill. The waters of the Pecos were reddened with the blood of Burketts. The quicksand of the Río Grande held the bodies of three Waldrons. Hired killers reaped their harvest or died cursing their luck. Outsiders kept clear of the feud. Neither side called in the law and the law did not interfere. Only the Burketts and the Waldrons knew the count of those who died. The Waldrons had left that war-torn strip and taken refuge among the outlaws who roamed that lawless section known as No Man's Land. Behind them were burned cabins and miles of barbed-wire fences cut between each pair of posts. In Texas men called that feud the Wire-Cutters' War.

John Moss stepped to the door, nodding brief greetings to the five horsemen.

"We follered Barlow Burkett here," said the tallest of the three Waldron cousins, Lash Waldron. "Where is the ol' he-wolf?"

"If you came here to take Barlow Burkett," said John Moss coldly, "you are doomed to disappointment."

"We rode a long ways to stretch his hide, mister."

"And he rode a long way to keep you from doing something like that. There'll be no murder done here."

"We rode a long ways," came the sullen repetition. A clotted bandage showed under Lash Waldron's hat. "Us Waldrons is in the habit of gittin' what we aim at."

Five grimy hands were resting on five cedar gun butts. Five pairs of bloodshot eyes glinted in the first rays of the sunrise,

"I have no gun," said John Moss. "I never use a gun. There is nothing to prevent your shooting me down in accordance with your customary methods of argument.

159

But before you kill me and the wounded man in my house, weigh this in your brains. To return to your home range you must first cross a fifty-mile strip of rough country. You were watched as you came in. You are being watched now. Harm me or mine and not a man of you will live to reach home. You men know who I am. You know that I tell you the truth."

"You got your own cause fer wantin' Barlow Burkett killed, John Moss. Don't deny it."

"I have cause to hate Barlow Burkett," admitted John Moss. "For the injury he did me, he'll pay dearly. But the man came here wounded. I'd do as much for a stray wolf. Put up your horses and have breakfast. But there will be no shooting. Your guns will be hung on the pegs. This is a house of friendship. You must not violate this threshold of peace. As men of peace you are welcome here. Otherwise, there lies the trail that leads to where you live."

For several moments the men eyed one another in questioning silence. Not a word was spoken, yet these tight-lipped men seemed to reach a conclusion. Lash Waldron again acted as spokesman.

"We'll be a-goin' back, Moss. When we're ready, we'll git that danged ol' he-wolf of the Burkett tribe. An' git this, Mister Psalm Singer. Don't let us git the chance tuh line our sights on your brisket when you cross the Flyin' W range. Fer if you set foot on our place, you'll turn up missin'."

He swung his tired horse around and rode off, the others following.

160

John Moss watched the five men out of sight. His clear blue eyes were clouded with brooding thought. The veins on his clenched hands stood out like purple cords. Then he turned and entered the house, the Ranch of the Four Winds, where even his bitterest enemy had found haven.

CHAPTER
TWO

Two weeks later Barlow Burkett was able to ride a horse. He sat in the living room, a trifle ill at ease. On the opposite side of the wide hearth sat the buckskin figure of John Moss. It was a man's room, filled with bright-colored Indian rugs, tanned lion and bear hides, shelves of books, tobacco jars and pipes. Old rusty guns and Indian relics decorated the walls. Here and there was an old English print; set in the stone masonry above the mantel was a bronze shield with a coat of arms and a Latin inscription. Across the shield was a bar — the Bar Sinister. Though these people of the frontier knew nothing of the marks and taints of heraldry, they felt that somehow this shield, with its inscription they could not read and its black diagonal bar, had to do with the presence of the tall Briton in this lawless land.

"I was listening, John Moss, when you sent the Waldrons away. You made enemies outta some powerful ornery snakes when you did it. You a-hating me like pizen, too. I never took much stock in religion, for I ain't never met the sky pilot yet that practiced his preachings. That is, till I heard you talk to Lash Waldron. And you don't claim to be no preacher."

"Far from it, Burkett. But a man doesn't necessarily have to be a gospel singer to practice a few of God's laws."

"Ain't there something in the Book about love thy enemy?" Old Barlow Burkett's left eyebrow quirked inquiringly.

"There is, Burkett. But I'd be lying if I claimed to feel anything but hatred for you. I kept Lash Waldron from killing you. But that's no indication of love for you on my part. I have cause to hate you, Barlow Burkett. You found me when my horse had been shot by either your outfit or the Waldrons. It was forty miles to the nearest water. But you laughed at me, called me a tenderfoot meddler, and rode off, leaving me to die. Recall that incident?"

"I do." The eyes of the old he-wolf of the Burkett clan now lighted up. "And you told me that you'd live because you wanted that day to come when you had me in as bad a fix." Burkett nodded, his tight lips twisting in a reminiscent smile. "I didn't think a human lived that could make that fifty miles afoot. Yet you did it. When I sent a man out next morning, he said you'd got home. He lost your sign and circled up on Desolation. He sighted you at your gate."

"Why did you send a man out after me, Burkett?"

"I'm ornery, John Moss, but not that ornery. I sent him with grub and water. Killing a man with a gun is one thing. Letting him die choking of black thirst is another. Besides, you ain't a Waldron."

"I didn't know that end of it, Burkett. For five years now I've thought of you as a man who would let a

163

fellow man die of thirst when it was within your power to save that man's life. I owe you an apology. It makes me glad I kept Lash Waldron from killing you."

The steel-colored eyes under the old he-wolf's heavy brows crinkled. There was something admirable about the cold courage of the grim-lipped feudist who spoke no word of the gnawing grief in his heart. No word of his murdered sons and wife passed his thin lips. Only in the mistiness of his brooding eyes, staring into the fire, had John Moss read that bitter grief eating like a cancer into the heart of the old he-wolf.

"I reckon," said Burkett, "the Injuns picked you up that evening, eh, Moss?"

The Briton shook his head, a soft smile on his lips. But he did not answer the question in the old cowman's glance. For it had been a girl who had found him and given him water and helped him across the desert. She was the most beautiful girl that John Moss had ever seen, as fair as a desert flower in May — black hair, blue eyes so dark that the twilight made them almost black. Her skin was that pink and white that belongs to Kerry. Even before he heard her laugh, John Moss knew her to be Irish. Yet when she spoke, she addressed him in an Indian language. Her clothes were of buckskin, beaded and quilled. She rode bareback with only a hackamore on her horse. But she would not speak English or Spanish nor would she tell him who she was or where she lived.

He had never seen her again. The Indians would not reveal the secret of her parentage or her home. When they had arrived at John Moss's home, she had whirled her horse and was gone. But her face lingered in the man's memory. If it is possible for a man to fall in love with a vision that haunts his fireside hours, then Sir John Moss was in love with the memory of her beauty.

As the two men sat by the log fire, wrapped in silence, old Barlow Burkett covertly watched the face of his host. Finally the old he-wolf broke that silence.

"Sooner or later the Waldrons'll get me. I'm a-going back to fight 'em." And again silence fell over them. John Moss smoked, his eyes thoughtful.

"When I rode here," Burkett went on, "thinking I was making my last ride, I didn't come hunting the protection of the Ranch of the Four Winds. I wa'n't scared to die. But there was something on my mind. If I died, I wanted you to know. That was why I had to live till I got here."

John Moss looked at his companion. The white-haired old feudist seemed rather uncertain how to solve the problem in his mind.

"Sooner or later, they'll get me. When they do, and after I'm dead, there's something I want to tell you. But a dead man can't talk. Now if I was to put it in writing and leave it here, you could put that letter away somewheres. When you see my dead body, you could read that letter. Not till then. Will you gimme your word not to open that letter till you've seen me dead, John Moss?"

"Of course. Write the letter and seal it. I'll put it away in my strongbox. When I have seen your dead body, I'll open it."

Burkett rose, bracing his injured leg against the chair. John Moss was also on his feet, held by the strange light in the older man's gray eyes.

"Swear it by that shield up yonder above the fireplace, Sir John Moss . . . by them words up yonder."

A crooked smile disfigured the mouth of the Briton, as his eyes fastened their gaze on the smoke-blackened shield, the shield with its black Bar Sinister — the taint of shame on a noble house. Slowly his lips translated the Latin motto of the House of Moss: "Death Before Dishonor."

"That's it." The old he-wolf nodded. "Swear it."

"You know the significance of the black bar across the shield?"

"Damn the black bar. Swear it!"

"By the honor of my father, his father, and his father's father," spoke Sir John Moss solemnly, "I swear to keep faith with you."

"Amen to that. Now if you'll fetch me pen and paper, I'll write it down."

John Moss guided him to writing desk, where pens, paper, and envelopes were in abundance. There was a stick of red sealing wax there.

For an hour the scratch of a laborious pen was the only sound that broke the silence. The buckskin figure of the host sat sprawled before the log fire. The odor of melting wax penetrated the haze of tobacco smoke.

John Moss fetched his strongbox and unlocked it. Into it Barlow Burkett placed the large, sealed envelope, face up. Across its face was written: **Barlow Burkett. To be opened after his death.**

166

John Moss closed the box and locked it.

"Now," said the white-haired old he-wolf, "I can die in peace. I'll be taking a Waldron or two along to hell with me when I go."

CHAPTER
THREE

Save for the old Indian woman, the Ranch of the Four Winds was empty of human voice. For John Moss was away on one of his frequent journeys. He would return in a day — or a week, or a month. His route or the nature of his journey was a mystery. It was as if some unseen hand beckoned and he answered its call. Always he rode alone, unarmed, astride a blood-bay horse that combined the gentleness of a dog with the stout gameness of a wild mustang.

Across mountains and desert, into towns and across wilderness. Camping alone or with the Indians. Lingering, smoking, talking. But always with a queer light behind his eyes. In towns he scanned the faces of every man. His aimless wanderings assumed the garb of a nameless quest, as if he were seeking someone or something and never found it, yet always hoping that the end of his search lay over the next horizon. Nor was it the face of the white Indian girl that beckoned. For ten years before he saw her, John Moss had made these journeys. Always he returned to the Ranch of the Four Winds, weary, gaunt, his eyes dulled with futility. But in a few weeks he would ride once more in search of that which he desired, that which had to do with the bronze shield that bore the black Bar Sinister.

Sometimes men awaited his return, their guns on the pegs in the entrance hall, strange men, roughly garbed, clumsy of speech. They ate and slept and smoked and waited till John Moss returned. His hospitality was too sacred a thing for violation. Outlaw and renegade respected it. The squaw fed them. And when he returned home, John Moss would hear their stories.

Moccasined feet padded softly about the house, the Indians' child-like curiosity in their eyes, gazing at the books and pictures, gazing raptly in awed silence at the bronze shield above the mantel. They took that to be the symbol of John Moss's god. They were not far from erring in that. Tradition and honor can be not unlike the Commandments of God.

So John Moss was gone on another journey, his eyes on the skyline, the big bay gelding eating up the miles at a running walk. At sundown he camped at a water hole at the edge of the cedar brakes of the Kaibab Forest. His evening meal consisted of coffee, jerked meat, and cold biscuits. The big bay, which he called Scarlet, grazed nearby without picket line or hobbles.

His frugal meal finished, John Moss squatted by the fire, his pipe between his teeth, a silent, motionless figure, wrapped in brooding thought. A worried frown puckered his eyes. For four days he had been traveling. On each of those days he had caught brief glimpses of a rider that always vanished from sight before Moss could focus his binoculars.

He was accustomed to the distant, watchful eyes of the Indians who often trailed him from curiosity or with some idea of protecting this man who was their friend. But this vanishing rider was no Indian. John Moss was certain of that. He knew an Indian as far as the eye could see. This man sat his horse like a cowpuncher. Once the sunlight had reflected the bits of silver decorations on the bridle and spurs.

When an Indian followed John Moss, it meant nothing but a sort of dog-like friendliness. But it is well to beware of a white man who follows one's trail with an apparent reluctance to reveal his identity.

Darkness had dropped its thick mantle across the cedars. Scarlet became a blurred shadow against the background of foliage. The campfire became a bed of dull red coals.

Suddenly, without warning, the scream of a woman shattered the quiet night. Once again came that scream of terror.

John Moss was on his feet, rigid, listening, as the last faint echo of the scream thinned to ominous silence. It had come from somewhere in the distance — half a mile, perhaps. Sound carries far in the high, rarefied air.

Then, as John Moss started through the forest of cedars, a single shot cracked, echoed, and left the silence, heavy and sinister. John Moss was running as fast as the uneven ground permitted. His moccasins made no noise as his steel-muscled legs carried his lithe body through the trees.

On and on he dodged, twisting through thickets, racing across open parks, never losing his point of direction. He was regretting his habit of going unarmed. Ahead lay a little park, silvery in the white light of a rising moon. In the center of the clearing lay a huddled body and another figure bending over it. Heedless of danger, John Moss covered the open space. The bending figure straightened. It was the buckskin-clad white girl of his dreams.

"He is dead," she said in clear English.

John Moss recovered from his surprise at seeing her, to bend over the dead man. It was Lash Waldron. A gun was clutched in his stiffening fingers. There was a dark bullet hole between his eyes.

"He is dead," repeated the girl dully.

"Quite," agreed John Moss. "Who shot him?"

"I do not know."

"It was you who screamed?" he asked, breathing heavily from his long run. The girl nodded. He saw that she was badly frightened. Also, her beaded buckskin dress was torn at the shoulder, revealing the creamy, white skin beneath.

"This man attacked you?" he asked, a strange, brittle harshness in his tone.

"Yes." She shuddered a little and her hands were busy trying to fasten the ripped dress. "I screamed. I was fighting him when a man rode across the clearing. He called out a name . . . Lash Waldron. This man, Waldron, shoved me away and I saw a gun in his hand. Then the man on the horse shot once and this man

171

dropped down and lay quiet, just as you see him, with the moonlight on his face."

"And the man who killed Lash Waldron?"

"Rode off as quickly as he had come, without a word."

"You would know his face if you saw him again?" asked John Moss.

"His face was hidden by a black handkerchief. No, I would not know him."

"And what brings you here?"

"I was trailing you," she said simply, and smiled a little.

"Why?"

"Because I had nothing else to do. I have often followed you. Sometimes I have slept near your camps."

"Without Scarlet giving alarm? Impossible."

"Scarlet?"

"My horse."

She laughed softly. "Long ago he and I made friends."

"*Hmmm*. I see. And you watched me, eh? Why?"

"To learn the ways of white men. My people tell me that you are a good white man, a chief whose lodge is a lodge of peace where white men and Indians smoke the pipe of peace, blowing the smoke to the four winds . . . a council lodge. So my foster father does not scold when I follow. He says no one can harm me when you are near because your medicine is good."

"And what about tonight? This beast could have killed you before I came."

"But you *did* come. It was you who killed him."

"I?"

"Who else, then?"

"Well, it was not I who came in time. Besides, I never carry a gun. You have someone else to thank."

But doubt still lingered in her eyes. "This man who died was following you to kill you." She spoke with firm conviction. "I have watched him. He would have killed you but he knew that eyes watched him and he was afraid. Tonight he was too quick for me and laid a trap. He caught me."

"You mean Lash Waldron has been trailing me to kill me?"

The girl nodded. "But each time he got ready, I shot an arrow near him and he was afraid to shoot you."

"That's interesting, eh? The coyotes won't bother him tonight. I'll send someone to bury him in the morning. Let's quit this spot. Have you eaten?"

"Not today."

"Then I'll ask you to share what I have."

"Thank you. I am very hungry," she accepted simply.

"The last time we met you spoke no English. Now you do."

"I had not learned so well then and was ashamed. I did not know then what I know now. I had always thought I was Sioux. Then I found that Eagle Chief was not my father and that I am not even a half-breed, like Antoine. I am white. So I made them let me learn my own tongue."

"Sioux, eh?" John Moss's eyes were burning brightly. "There are Sioux here in Arizona? A Sioux named Eagle Chief? That's why I never found you. You do not

173

live with the Moki tribes, the Hopi or Zuñni people. Tell me, what brings a Sioux warrior here?"

"Does the White Fawn ask why John Moss lives here?" she rebuked him gently.

"I beg your pardon. Didn't mean to be rude. You are White Fawn?"

"Yes. Even Eagle Chief does not tell me my other name. Antoine is no better. Antoine laughs and says someday I shall know."

"And who is Antoine?"

"The half-breed who describes himself as . . . 'The strongest damn' man in all Quebec.' He teaches me the language of my white father who was a soldier and a gentleman. Only sometimes I do not know which are the bad words that ladies do not say. Like what I said about the 'strongest damn' man in all Quebec.' That is a little joke. Always Antoine makes the joke because he says when I laugh it makes him think of a girl up at Quebec. But when I ask Eagle Chief, he says that Antoine is a very big liar and never saw Quebec. Then Antoine laughs all the more and says perhaps that was his brother who went to Quebec. And he sings very loud and then very soft, like the wind in the pines. He sings in French, very gay and very happy. But I have seen him sometimes when his heart is on the ground and he is sad."

"*Hmmm*. A very interesting chap. Handsome, no doubt?"

"Very handsome and strong. He can set a bear trap with his two hands."

They reached John Moss's camp and he threw wood on the coals of his fire. Scarlet let the girl rub his nose and ears. John Moss, preparing the inadequate meal for her, frowned perplexedly into the blaze. A Sioux here among the Hopi tribe was indeed strange. What of this Antoine fellow — Antoine, who was so fond of music and laughter and could set a bear trap with his hands? John Moss doubted that latter accomplishment. He decided that Antoine was a braggart Cree half-breed. Quebec, eh? Quebec. And this white girl whose father's name was a secret. Quebec — and beyond that city of French and Indians and English, a thousand miles westward by train and canoe and dog team, the immense wilderness controlled by the great fur company, Hudson's Bay Company, a company of gentlemen adventurers. In his mind, John Moss followed that thousand-mile trail. Quebec, due West and skirting Lake Abitibi, to Long Lake. Winnipeg. Portage la Prairie. Regina and Medicine Hat. Then north and farther north. Into the snow-swept isolation of Peace River, white and silent and sinister. Creaking sled-runners. Frosty breath of a husky team. A snowshoe track in a white wilderness. A scarlet splash on the white shroud of the North country where a man of Canada's famous Mounted Police had died with a bullet in his back. The death howl of a Malamute dog in the frozen night of a Slave Lake winter.

Memory of that terrible trek across the frozen wilderness clouded the eyes of John Moss. Proof of that journey was stamped in a black Bar Sinister across the shield of Moss with its brave words: "Death Before Dishonor." Proof of that dishonor that tainted a proud

175

name lay in a frozen grave. But John Moss still had a vow to fulfill, a debt of honor to pay, a mystery to solve — a life to give in payment of a life taken by another man. That man had been John's father, Sir Edward Moss, who had vanished into the white maw of that terrible silence of the North country — Sir Edward Moss, whose trail lay hidden by the wind that swept the white snow across his sled tracks.

A letter had awaited John Moss, given to him by an Indian who came and vanished. It was unsigned, unsealed, cryptic in its wording — a letter that had sent John Moss back to civilization. It was in an unfamiliar handwriting, too, as full of mystery as the white blaze of the Northern Lights — a message of death, a warning, yet a message that carried a line of hope:

That man whom you seek is dead. That which he set out to accomplish is as hopeless as it remains heroic. Let not youth judge the methods of his task but rather cherish only the memory of a brave death, a death that lifted a futile dream to the heights of a thing sublime. There shall be a more splendid judgment that places no Bar Sinister across the shield of that man who, when he faced the supreme test, placed Death Before Dishonor. Would to God this world held more men like him.

The answer to your quest lies not where his body rests from its labors. Seek you a land where there is a shield older by many hundred years than that shield across which lies the Bar Sinister — a sun shield, round, containing four colors. Each color represents a compass point. Where the red waters of the Colorado fall through a giant gorge. Where its cañon walls are painted many colors. Where civilization was old when Christ was born.

Go there and build your home. You are young. By listening to the old men among the Indians you may learn that which you seek. They are a people of peace who pray to that sun shield. They will judge you. If you prove worthy, you shall learn the answer to many things. Perhaps, John Moss, you will then know in your heart that the laws of God are greater than the laws of King or President, of Parliament or Senate. And in the wisdom of that knowledge well learned, there shall be no Bar Sinister across the shield of Moss.

Recall you those lines of the Bard of Avon? —

Nothing in his life became him like
The leaving of it.
He died as one who
Studied, in his death, to throw away
The most precious thing he owned
As 'twere a careless trifle.

So did Sir Edward Moss, gentleman and soldier, cast aside that which he valued more than life — his honor. So I, who was his friend, advise John, his son, to withhold judgment. And if you can say, when your time to die is at hand: "I am as was my father," then I will add this: "*You are a man!*"

177

John Moss, staring into the blaze of his campfire, recalled the words of that letter that now lay in his strongbox. In some vague manner this girl in beaded buckskin was linked with that frozen secret of Slave Lake and the Peace River wilderness, with that Sioux warrior, Eagle Chief, with the half-breed, Antoine, who spoke of Quebec. All were bits in this unsolved puzzle. The Hopi people of the Painted Desert, their kivas, their symbols, their sun shield, the dark eyes that held secrets of things unspoken in their opaque depths — eyes that followed John Moss, eyes that dwelt on the bronze shield with its black bar of shame, eyes that watched his campfires — old eyes, shadowed with unspoken thoughts. Something told John Moss that the end of his long quest was soon to come; that this girl and her two companions fitted into its solution; that here, within a day's ride of the Grand Cañon of the muddy Colorado, here where summer sun blazed without mercy on a sand-strewn desert, lay the end of a journey that had begun in the snow-blanketed wilderness of the far North.

"You look very sad, friend." The girl's voice roused John Moss.

"Sad?" He straightened his wide shoulders and smiled as he lifted the blackened little coffee pot from the coals. "Not sad. Thoughtful, rather. I'm sorry I haven't more in the way of food."

He liked the white flash of her quick smile. Then his eyes caught the glitter of some little token that was fastened about her white throat by a buckskin thong. As she bent over to take the cup of black coffee from his

178

hand, the trinket dangled within a few inches of his face. With a quick gasp of astonishment, he reached it with his hand and bent to study it. The object was a man's gold signet ring. The ring bore the crest of Moss. But no Bar Sinister marred its engraved surface. It had been twenty years since John Moss, a mere boy, had seen that ring on the hand of Sir Edward Moss, his father.

"Where did you get this ring?" he whispered huskily.

"It was my father's," she said in a low tone that quivered a little at the man's intense interest that was more than idle curiosity.

"Your father's ring?" His eyes, like twin burning blue fires, studied her face. Was this girl his half-sister? Was Sir Edward Moss her father?

"You are positive that this ring belonged to your father?"

"Yes. Please don't look at me so. It frightens me."

"I . . . I beg your pardon. God knows I did not mean to frighten you. You can't know how . . . what it means to me, finding this ring, you know. Tell me, won't you, please, what you know about your father?"

"There is little to tell. He is dead. He was a very brave man. Brave and kind. He lived far North where the snow is deep and where the Indians drive dogs hooked to a sled. That is all. He is dead."

"Your mother? Is she also dead?"

"Yes. Dead of a broken heart, Antoine says. That is all I know."

"I'll get the rest from Antoine," said John Moss grimly, "Antoine and Eagle Chief."

White Fawn smiled softly into the flickering firelight.

179

CHAPTER
FOUR

Barlow Burkett, the old he-wolf of his clan, sat smoking before the grate fire in the Ranch of the Four Winds. He had been there several hours when John Moss, riding alone, reached home.

"Howdy, John Moss."

"You beat me home," replied the tall Briton. He found a bottle and two glasses. "Drink?"

"Don't mind if I do." Burkett smiled. "What became of the White Fawn?"

"She slipped away from me after supper," growled Moss, wondering how Burkett came by the knowledge of her name.

Burkett nodded. "That Lash Waldron needed killing shore bad. Here's wishing you luck, John Moss."

"You saved her life, Burkett," said John Moss when they set down their empty glasses.

"She ain't for Lash Waldron," said the old he-wolf almost fiercely. "Nor no other Waldron nor their breed. Kinda comical, that parade towards the Kaibab. Her trailing you, Lash following you to bushwhack you, and me bringing up the drag, watching the whole play. And there was times when I thought there was an Injun trailing me." He chuckled to himself.

180

John Moss was pacing the room with restless tread. The old cowman watched him covertly, a queer twinkle in his eyes.

"You know, John Moss," he said musingly, "the more I see of white people, the more I respect an Injun. I reckon you are the only white man I know that I'd trust outta sight. I've lived among Injuns for the past forty years. When I come to this country from Texas, I didn't have a friend, an extra pair of socks, or bed to lay in. Just a half-growed kid. I'd just come from a slaughter among my folks and the Waldrons. I had a bullet hole or two in my hide. I was fourteen years old, John Moss, but there was three fresh notches on the old rifle I packed. There was a couple of Waldron men trailing me when I cut acrost the desert. They gave up at the edge of the desert. Scared to chance it for lack of water. No wonder. My horse died of thirst. I was damn' nigh dead when I dropped at the mouth of Cañon de Chelly, as it's now called. A Zuñi runner found me. He packed me to the pueblo at Walpi, where they brought me back to life. I lived on the Painted Desert with the Injuns for ten years. Those folks sure can keep a secret. Sometimes it seems to a white man that they carry a secret too long. But most likely they find they got some good reason for keeping quiet."

John Moss had halted and stood there, looking down at Burkett, who sprawled in a big chair, smoking, his eyes looking into the fire.

"Are you trying to tell me something?" asked John Moss.

181

"I'm older'n you," said Burkett without looking up. "When a man gets old, he learns the value of patience. If I was you, I wouldn't try to find the White Fawn till her folks is ready for you to locate their home. You couldn't find the spot in fifty years unless you had a guide. When the time comes, you'll find her. You'll find the answer to other things."

The keen gray eyes of the old killer glanced upward, resting their gaze on the bronze shield with the black Bar Sinister.

"In heaven's name, man, what do you mean?" cried John Moss.

"I have spoken," grunted Barlow Burkett.

"Another riddle. By gad, I'm going to find the answer."

"Easy, pardner," rumbled the white-haired old Texan. "You ain't winning nothing going off half-cocked. When the time comes, you'll find what you came here to find. But you'll die wondering if you start gunning for information. Injuns're odd folks. Peaceful, shore. But their gods kinda work queer things. I've seen men die because they crossed the Injun gods. I knew that when you got back here you'd be raring to make a hunt. So I laid over to have a medicine talk with you."

"You know where White Fawn lives?" asked John Moss tensely.

Burkett shook his head. "Don't be a darn' fool."

"I'm hitting the trail in the morning. I'm going to follow that trail to its end."

"The end is here . . . here in this room." Barlow Burkett's long, gnarled trigger finger pointed to the bronze shield with its coat of arms. "Up there, Sir John Moss."

"What do you mean?"

"That black bar acrost it. Pride is a hell of a curse, John Moss. Because a King or Queen says your daddy was a skunk and puts that black stripe acrost his brand, kinda venting it, you side in with 'em. You take the word of some Canadian sheriff that yore daddy was a snake. You abide by their decision. Why?"

"Because I saw proof," said John Moss bitterly.

"Yeah? Don't be too certain. A man's eyes can lie to him. I've been fooled that-a-way. What was that proof?"

"A dead man in the snow with a bullet in his back. The dead man was a Mountie following him to arrest him for rank disloyalty to the Crown. Poaching on land where he had no right. Inciting the Indians to rebellion. Breaking faith with the government that employed him."

"And did it ever occur to you, John Moss, that a government can be wrong? Ever stop to think that your daddy might have some other reason besides money or power, when he spits in the Queen's eye and swaps his title and standing with the government for an Injun teepee and a grave in a snowbank?"

"What do you know about my father?" said John Moss, who stood there a little white about the lips.

"Nothing except this . . . that he was a game son-of-a-gun, one man against a government. You heard their side of the story. You've taken the words of some lawman dressed up in pretty red monkey jackets. You

183

stood in some office and let 'em call your daddy a crook."

"I managed to knock down the man who blackguarded his name," said John Moss quietly, "and three or four other officers who blocked my way out."

"That's better. Then you never really believed your dad was a skunk."

"Hardly, Burkett. My job is to clear his name, to wipe away the Bar Sinister. Would I be here if I thought my father was the traitor they claim him to be?"

"When the Injuns are positive that your heart is right, my friend, they'll come here to the Ranch of the Four Winds. The White Fawn will come with 'em. It's like I said, they're apt to be too cautious. Us white fellers ain't as patient as they are. We can't set down and wait. But we'd be a better race if we could."

"I've sat here ten years and more," spoke John Moss. "I'm hitting the trail tomorrow."

"Then I'm afraid you'll die without ever knowing the end of the story. Those Injun gods're bad medicine. Kachinas, they call 'em. Well, I gotta be drifting."

"But it's bedtime. You're staying all night."

"Nope. I do most of my riding of a night. The Waldrons're out after my scalp. They're gonna be shore riled up over Lash. Wish you'd change your mind about hunting the girl and her folks."

John Moss smiled stubbornly. "I'm tired of waiting."

"Well, pack a gun when you leave here. The Waldrons each has a bullet named for you. Pack a gun and plenty cartridges."

"I will," said John Moss grimly. "You've given me something to think about, Burkett. Don't think I'm not appreciative. I'm not going to ask you how you happen to know so much about my father. You're bound to silence and you've told me all you can. I won't do anything foolish. And I'll keep my eyes open for the Waldrons. They're using you as an excuse to get me. They've never liked me. I've had one or two threats from them the past years."

"They're snakes. To make it worse, they've managed to get Sim Waldron elected sheriff at Hackberry. Sim's sworn in his tribe as deputies. They're rustling cattle wholesale. Just about cleaned me out. They've put a big price on my head. I'm an outlaw. Lash was a deputy and that'll make it all the worse for me. That's why I'm riding nights and hiding days. Coyote-running into the badlands. Picking off all I can afore they get me. Once a man begins killing, he's gotta keep his hand in. But with maw and the boys gone, it don't make much difference now. Well, see you when we meet again, John Moss. It's good to know a real man. So long."

And Barlow Burkett, the fighting old he-wolf, took his departure. He rode off into the night, a lonely figure of hate, the last of his killer clan. Like a wolf he was, hunted by a hound pack, white-maned, snarling, hating as he fought and ran and fought again. His heart was eaten with bitterness, his brain warped with the cunning of a killer, prowling through the starlight, hiding away by the light of day. It was but a matter of time until he should make his last stand against the pack, until he should die fighting, like a snapping, snarling, killing he-wolf.

When his visitor had gone, John Moss paced the room, driven to restlessness by chaotic thoughts. Now and then he paused, staring up at the bronze coat of arms. Finally, with a muttered ejaculation, he brought out the heavy steel strongbox and opened it with a small key. From the box he took a stack of folded papers fastened with a broad elastic band. He sat down before the fire, studying a yellowed letter from the pile that lay in his lap. It was the letter given him by the Indian that night many years ago at Slave Lake. He read it over and over, studying it.

So engrossed in his study was John Moss that he did not see the face that stared in at the window behind him — a face hidden by the night, barely discernible from within. For long minutes he studied the letter and some other papers. Then he rose to replace the papers in the box. On the long table beside the box lay Barlow Burkett's sealed letter. Moss picked it up, idly curious. Then he started, a little exclamation of surprise on his lips. For the red seals were stamped with the seal of Moss, the shield of the House of Moss. But no Bar Sinister marred the seal, stamped plainly in the red wax.

The house was quiet as a tomb. No sound came from the kitchen. The crackling of the fire sounded strangely loud in the stillness. And John Moss, his fine hands trembling a little, stared at the sealed envelope that he now knew held some secret concerning the fate of his father. The ring worn by White Fawn had stamped those red seals. Then Barlow Burkett had come here to the Ranch of the Four Winds to reveal that secret before he died. The he-wolf had sought to do John Moss a favor. He recalled Burkett's words, something about the Indians carrying a secret too long. Temptation to rip open the envelope was almost overpowering. But he had given his oath not to open the letter until he saw Burkett's dead body. He restored the letter to the box and was picking up the other letters when a bullet crashed through the window and buried itself in the log wall by the fireplace.

John Moss knocked out the light and sprang for the door. Even as he sprang, an agonized cry of a man in mortal agony came from the night outside.

In the little entrance hall, John Moss groped along the wooden pegs and found his six-shooter. The gun in his hand, he leaped out into the darkness. A blot of a shadow vanished around the corner of the long log house. Under the window lay a writhing body. The Briton kneeled beside the dying man, peering into the distorted face.

The man went suddenly limp, eyes wide, glazing with death. Something wet and sticky fouled John Moss's probing hands. The man who had lain outside and shot through the window at Moss had been stabbed in the back.

There was sound of movement inside the house. The next moment the old squaw appeared carrying a lantern, a squat, calico figure filling her kitchen doorway. She made no outcry.

"Put out that light!" called John Moss. She obeyed without a word. "Get inside. Bolt the doors. Don't open up for anyone but me!" he told her. Then, running silently on moccasined feet, he rounded the house.

It was an hour before he returned. He had found a saddled horse in a piñon thicket behind the corrals. But beyond that horse, which was the one ridden by the man who now lay dead under the window, Moss had found nothing. The horse wore the Flying-W brand on the left shoulder. The dead man was either a Waldron or one of the Waldrons' hired killers.

The dead man in his arms, John Moss strode to the kitchen door and called. The old squaw admitted him. She showed no trace of surprise or fright.

"Get a light," he said gruffly. "We'll have a look at this fellow."

The squaw lit the lantern again and held it so that its light fell on the face of the dead man whose body lay on the floor.

"One of the men that was with Lash Waldron the day they came after Burkett," he recalled. "Took a pot shot at me. Why didn't he come closer at such short range? That knife must have stabbed him as he lined his sights. But who the devil knifed him? Barlow Burkett? Hardly. A gun is Burkett's way. Or is the old he-wolf a knifeman as well as a gunman?" After all, he knew little of Burkett's methods of fighting. Perhaps an Indian had done it. He now questioned the squaw: "Did you see anyone around that might have killed this man?"

"No." The old squaw looked with evident distaste at the blood on her scrubbed floor. "Takem outside now?"

"We'll put the body out in the woodshed till morning. Take his feet. I'll carry his upper body."

So they carried out the dead man, their passage marked by a dripping trail of blood. They shut the shed door on its grisly occupant and John Moss washed his hands while the squaw set about cleaning her floor. Her muttering complaint brought a faint smile to Moss's lips. What white woman could be so callous to death?

He drew heavy curtains across the living room windows and lit his pipe. Idly he resumed the restoration of his papers to the strongbox. Midway in the task he paused. For a long moment he stood there, pipe gripped between his teeth, his eyes bent on the half-filled box. He distinctly recalled placing all save one packet of papers back in the box. Yet there on the table, spread out as if someone had hastily pawed through them, were papers that should have been neatly piled at the bottom of the box. Someone had been in this room while he was outside.

Barlow Burkett's sealed letter was missing. The letter that held John Moss's secret, the letter sealed with the coat of arms of Moss, was gone.

CHAPTER
FIVE

There was little sleep for John Moss that night. His rigid questioning of the squaw, who he always called Pocahontas — usually abbreviated to Poky — availed him nothing. Her old face was as blank as always of expression. She was either a marvelous liar or extraordinarily stupid. His questions brought grunts and head shakings. His systematic search of the house revealed no hidden person.

The two startling facts remained, however. A dead man lay in the woodshed. The sealed letter had vanished. John Moss paced the floor, stopping now and then to examine the bullet hole in the window, trying to piece together bits of this odd puzzle of drama.

Had the man who killed the Waldron gunman slipped into the house and stolen the letter? If so, why? Of what value to anyone was that document? Had Barlow Burkett been the killer and thief? Had the old he-wolf regretted that letter and returned to steal it? And, finding an enemy at the window, had he knifed the man? Or had some Indian done the killing? They kept a rather close watch on the Ranch of the Four Winds. Always they had been given the freedom of the house during John Moss's absence. This was the first time that any object had ever been stolen.

Whoever had stolen the letter was now in possession of certain knowledge that Barlow Burkett wished kept secret, knowledge that John Moss would have given anything to know. Now that paper and its precious contents were lost, possibly forever. In the hands of an enemy, that paper might be a powerful weapon. There was the little matter of a blot of scarlet on the snow, a murdered Mountie the mystery of whose death might be solved in the pages of that document. A dangerous weapon, indeed, in the hands of Burkett's enemies if, in those written pages, Barlow Burkett had revealed a secret of the Indians. Burkett had said that the gods of the Indians worked queer charms. It ill behooves a man to violate the confidence of the Hopi people. Ill luck befalls a traitor. What better weapon against Burkett could the Waldrons ask for?

The best course of action, John Moss mused, *is to find Barlow Burkett and tell him the letter is stolen. If he took it, well, he was simply reclaiming his own property. But if the Waldrons or some Indian lifted that letter from the box, God help the old he-wolf.*

John Moss was in the saddle at dawn, armed with a carbine and his old white-handled Colts. He seldom went armed, but as two men within the week had sought his life, he deemed it the act of a fool to go unarmed. Where to hunt for Burkett was a problem. As well hunt a wolf at large.

There was little of the superstitious about John Moss; he was a man of cold nerve, level-headed and unexcitable. Yet, as he quit Desolation Mesa and entered the fringe of cedars that dotted the rough country, a feeling of uneasiness crept up his spine. He caught himself listening, nerves taut, for sounds. His eyes swept the cedar thickets with a restless, wary glance. Scarlet, the big bay, minced along the trail, furry ears twitching. The horse seemed to sense the rider's wariness.

John Moss had felt that nameless dread of the mysterious before, up in the snowbound Slave Lake country, and that feeling of being watched by invisible eyes, always with death lurking like some skulking carrion beast, just out of sight in the shadow. Little sounds, never before noticed, whispered in the stillness. A twig snapped somewhere. A bird took flight without cause. A rabbit scurried across the trail, frightened by something. Little things noticeable to a man accustomed to the wilderness. Yet there was nothing there when the man looked. A broken twig. A bruised leaf. But no human being visible anywhere.

The man's nerves were on edge. He had dug a grave and buried a man that morning before daylight, a task that was sufficient in itself to blight one's day. And while he could not be positive, he was almost certain that someone had been in the shed, looking at the dead body of that man sometime during the night. The wooden pin in the door latch seemed to be in a different position. The tarpaulin that covered the body was awry. To add to the horror, there was the matter of the rats. John Moss had forgotten that the woodshed was the winter home of the huge wood rats. He

192

shuddered a little as he remembered the two that ran squealing from under the tarp when he and the squaw came to bury the man.

It was a gray day, a bleak wind whining across the cedars, cold, raw, hinting of snow. An owl, half blind in the daylight, careened across the treetops. An owl does not fly by day unless disturbed. With a soft curse, John Moss swung abruptly from the trail, and headed for the cedar thicket and the thick, red-branched manzanita brush beyond. A few minutes later man and horse fought their way back out of the tangle of brush. Nothing but an animal could have penetrated that thicket. Perhaps a lion or bobcat had disturbed the owl, or an Indian on foot. No Waldron, that was certain. The best brush hand in Arizona could not ride through that tangle.

For the first time since he had come to this country, John Moss felt an irritable impatience with the Indians. Why the devil did they have to be so secretive? Why did they watch his every move? Why couldn't they . . . ? John Moss quit musing to stare through narrowed eyes at a rider who came along the trail toward him — a white man who wore the leather jumper and bull-hide chaps of a cowpuncher, a man whose hand dropped to the butt of a big-calibered Colt as he recognized the buckskin-clad John Moss. A shiny badge adorned the flannel chest of the rider.

John Moss recognized the hawk-like face of Sim Waldron, brother of the dead Lash. He was the Waldron recently made sheriff of Hackberry. John Moss viewed the man with tightly compressed lips. Here, at least, was tangible evidence of enmity. The riders halted, a few feet separating their horses. John Moss scrutinized the face of Sim Waldron. Waldron had a quick start of surprise at seeing Moss. That look of surprise gave way to one of dark suspicion.

"Ridin' kinda early, ain't yuh, Moss?"

"I am. What of it?"

Sim Waldron's left hand touched his badge. "It's my business tuh learn what brings folks out on a cold mornin'. Must've left home afore sunup. Or was yuh home last night?"

"That concerns no man but myself, Waldron," said John Moss coldly. "A man's house is his own, to leave when and how he chooses. I've been warned to keep off the Flying-W range. When I trespass on your property, I'll take what comes. I may add, Sim Waldron, that it's rather bad luck for a Waldron to trespass on my property."

It was plain that Sim Waldron was eaten with curiosity regarding the whereabouts of the man who had last night visited the Ranch of the Four Winds. John Moss, on the other hand, was wondering how much Sim Waldron knew about the stolen letter.

"A damned skunk murdered my brother not far from here," said Sim Waldron. "I just come from buryin' Lash. I'm primed tuh kill the skunk that done fer Lash. If I figgered it was you, I'd gut-shoot yuh now."

"If you were fast enough with bull-hide chaps," added John Moss. "Lash died before he could pull the trigger. There's food for some thought in that little . . ."

John Moss's gun appeared in his hand. A moment before John Moss's two hands had rested idly on his saddle horn. Then, so swiftly that the movement was lost to the eye, a gun appeared in the Briton's hand. Its barrel now pointed steadily at Sim Waldron.

"Lash died before he could thumb the hammer of his gun. Be careful that you do not die of that same disease . . . lead poisoning, brought on by sluggish activity of the gun hand. Whoever killed Lash Waldron deserves a vote of thanks from the territory. Later, when proper legislation begins functioning, such beasts as Lash Waldron and his breed will be exterminated by an act of law. You can't bulldoze me, Waldron. I'm not to be frightened by such tactics as have been used in an effort to put out my light. Ponder on this. Lash Waldron, your erstwhile estimable brother, man of parts and murderer *par excellence*, sought to kill me. An unfortunate accident befell him that put an end to his bushwhacking game. A very promising career nipped in the old bud. His light was damned well obliterated. A man in your position, brother in blood and disposition, might well profit by the lesson of his undoing. Another gentleman of like promise as the deceased Lash, a creature of similar whims, habits, and general traits, who evidently nursed an obsession in common with the unfortunate Lash, paid a visit last night to the Ranch of the Four Winds. Sad to relate, the fellow's skill with firearms was not all that might be wished for. He was buried this morning." There was a cold, blue light in the eyes of John Moss as he watched Sim Waldron, a light that hinted of the powers of wrath beneath the

195

outward calm of the big Briton. "Death, they say, runs in a cycle of threes. Odd, is it not, that we should have met this morning? Damned odd, come to think of it. Eh?"

"You have the drop, Moss. Go ahead and shoot." Sim Waldron spat a stream of tobacco juice at a juniper bush. Whatever faults might taint the man's character, cowardice was not among them. And beneath that air of loose-muscled carelessness was a tensity that showed in the man's slitted, black eyes. Sim Waldron's claw-like hand still gripped his gun butt. Moss retained the advantage of the drop. A split second of laxity on the Briton's part meant sudden death.

"Unbuckle your gun belt, Waldron. Hang it on your saddle. Then step down on the ground. I'm going to do likewise. Then I'm going to attempt to beautify your cherubic countenance."

"Speak American, you lousy British dude!"

"Very well, my dear fellow. I'm going to beat hell out of you. Does that thing you call a mind grasp the meaning of those one-syllabled words? They tell me you're quite the bully of the neighborhood. Wrestler, fistfighter, so on. Let's have a try at you. Step down, you murderer."

"I kin savvy talk like that." Waldron grinned one-sidedly and again fouled the foliage with tobacco juice. Then he unbuckled his cartridge belt and stepped off his horse. Still grinning, he unbuckled his chaps. Then he pulled off his jumper and hat, spat on his hands, and leered up at John Moss, who was unbuckling his belt.

196

Sim Waldron, big-boned, heavy-shouldered, hard as rawhide, looked formidable enough. The open front of his flannel shirt revealed a breadth of hairy chest. As John Moss swung off onto the ground and faced him, the two were evenly matched in reach and weight, both hardened by outdoors life, quick in movement, fired with hatred.

CHAPTER
SIX

With a sudden snarl of fury, Sim Waldron leaped clear of the ground. His bulk thudded against John Moss, who was not prepared to meet the swift, unexpected onslaught. The Briton's hands had been busy unfastening the collar of his buckskin shirt. The men went down in a heap. But with a sudden twist, John Moss was on his feet again. There was a tiny trickle of blood at the corner of his mouth.

"Get up and fight!" he snapped.

Waldron was rising slowly, cautiously. It was the first time in the cowman's career as a rough-and-tumble fighter that a man, given the Briton's advantage, did not make an attempt to stomp a fallen foe. Instead, John Moss stood back, not even rushing when Waldron gained his feet.

They circled warily, eyes watching for an opening, Waldron a bit heavier on his feet than the moccasined Moss, who crouched, his jaw partly protected by his left shoulder, a minimum of his abdomen exposed. His feet were as nimble as those of a dancing master. He was smiling, cool, taunting in his manner. His insolence crazed Waldron. The effrontery of the Briton was appalling, unheard of.

"I'm gonna kill yuh afore I'm done!" gritted Waldron. "I'm gonna kill yuh . . ."

John Moss feinted, drew a swing from Waldron that he ducked, then at close range lifted the dark, scowling face with two swift uppercuts that dazed Sim, who bored in wildly, shaking his injured head like an enraged bull. And John Moss, standing aside, ripped slashing jabs into the rage-blackened face. But Waldron came on, fists hammering, trying to clench with the punishing foe that rocked his head with stiff jolts.

Here were no boxer's roped arena, no seconds or referee. No rules governed the fighters. Waldron was hitting low. Moss stabbed at the distorted face, smashing hard lefts at the bobbing head that was too slow to get away. One of Waldron's eyes was closing. A moment later a left hook smashed his nose, spattering him with blood. Blind with pain and blood, elation giving way to dogged determination, he followed Moss, who tried to keep out of range.

John Moss knew the danger of close fighting. He had seen men come out of such mêlées with an ear or nose bitten off or an eye gouged from its socket. Moss had no intention of fighting in that manner. He did not relish the thought of losing an eye or part of an ear. But it was hard to avoid those bellowing, bull-like rushes of Waldron.

Sim Waldron's red eyes followed the dancing Moss. His flailing fists were clipping closer now. He was deliberately swinging low, hoping to land a hard jolt to John Moss's groin. Never until now had a man stood up to John Moss's blows. Since boyhood John Moss had studied boxing. He once had fought for, and lost by the mere shadow of chance, the middleweight amateur championship of the British Isles. Older now, something of his agility and punching power was fading, but he was still a good man. Sim Waldron must be made of rubber and rawhide to stand up to him.

The cowman was taking punishment without a whimper. Swings and uppercuts rocked the man horribly. But he came on, dogged, bloody, battered beyond recognition. Then, with a short grunt of elation, he closed with Moss. The dancing feet no longer danced. It was the bulldog's turn. Waldron's knee shot up, its foul blow missing Moss's groin by a mere inch. Eyes closed to mere slits, torn lips bared from tobacco-stained fangs, Sim Waldron tripped Moss and fell heavily on top of him. And John Moss now lacked the fresh stamina to wriggle from under the fury-strengthened weight of Sim Waldron, whose battered, blood-smeared face, unshaven, distorted, horrible, came lower to sink animal-like teeth into Moss's face. Waldron's weight was on Moss's lower ribs. Waldron's vise-like hands pinioned Moss's weary arms. And the snarling, dripping, cursing face came closer to Moss's face, teeth parted and snapping like a dog's, the slitted eyes no longer human in their red hate. Both men were panting sobbingly from the terrible grueling they had undergone.

"Gonna . . . chaw . . . yore damn' face off!" Waldron slobbered blood and tobacco. His ugly face came closer.

200

Then Moss's legs shot up in a back somersault, shot up and crossed with a vicious crosswise grip under Waldron's chin, then back, like a lever, carrying the astounded Waldron backward. Flung off balance, Sim Waldron felt himself hurled aside by the steel-muscled legs of Moss. The next instant both men were again on their feet.

"Now, Waldron," panted John Moss. "Now we fight!"

No longer dancing out of range, no longer letting Waldron carry the fight, John Moss bored in. He was timing his punches with cold fury, advancing slowly, following the retreating Waldron, who for the first time showed fear. Moss kept smashing, jabbing, stabbing the battered face, the broken nose, the closing eyes of Sim Waldron, who fought like a whipped bulldog.

Jolted almost insensible, half blind from blood and sweat and pain and dirt, Sim Waldron staggered under the blows, kept his feet, and swung now and then in vain attempts to drop Moss with a low punch. Dirty fighter he might be, ready to take every advantage, yet there was no yellow streak in Sim Waldron. Few men could have taken the terrible punishment he was taking. Then Moss stepped to one side, cocked his left arm, and the spat of his fist dropped Sim Waldron like the blow of an axe.

For a long moment John Moss stood above the battered, motionless heap of the whipped man. Panting, blood-smeared, his face swollen and discoloring, the Briton's eyes held a look of sincere admiration for the fighting prowess of the crumpled Waldron.

201

Utterly exhausted, the big Briton sat there, his breath heaving his tortured, battered ribs, wiping away the blood from his face with a clean linen handkerchief. He half turned as Sim Waldron moaned through his torn mouth and slowly rose, swaying on his feet.

"Got enough, Waldron?" he called.

"Got aplenty fer now," admitted Sim Waldron, walking with unsteady gait toward the seated Briton. "Yo're a better man than Sim Waldron. I know when I'm whupped."

John Moss did not see the treacherous glint in the killer's eyes. He did not know that a Waldron was never beaten so long as life flickered in a Waldron heart. There was a granite rock the size of a baseball palmed in Sim Waldron's hairy paw.

"Yuh licked me all right, Moss," mumbled Sim Waldron, staggering like a drunken man. "I'm groggier'n hell yet. Yuh shore pack a kick in that left hand." The man's broken voice held a whine of defeat that threw Moss off his guard. Moreover, his unsteady legs and listless arms betokened complete lack of strength. Weaving unsteadily, he halted on widespread legs before the seated Moss and shoved out a grimy, blood-smeared right hand. "Here's my hand on it!"

Moss, half rising, smiled crookedly and took the proffered hand. The next instant the Briton was jerked off balance and the rock in Waldron's left hand thudded with a sickening force behind Moss's ear. John Moss sprawled forward on his face. A trickle of blood oozed across his inert face. Waldron threw the rock at the unconscious form, then, the stagger gone from his gait,

202

he crossed to his horse and jerked his gun from its belt that was looped over the saddle horn.

"Yo're overdue now," croaked Waldron, and advanced with the long-barreled .45 toward the Briton.

"*Bo' jou, m'sieu!*" boomed a deep voice. It came from the brush behind Waldron, who whirled to face a huge man whose cocked carbine pointed with disconcerting steadiness at Sim Waldron's chest. "She's bettair *pour* you, *m'sieu*, you drop de gon. Damn' queeck! Lak' dat. *Oui!* Now with the foot, keeck dat gon my way. So. *Merci!* Now get on de horse and ride *pour* long tam. Till you get home. Me, I'm purty bad feller when I'm get mad. Me, Antoine Fiant who set de bear trap weeth de two han's."

The newcomer was well over six feet and superbly built, with huge shoulders, trim waist, and long-muscled legs. He wore faded overalls, a thick flannel shirt, and high, moose-hide moccasins. No hat covered the thick mane that was white as driven stow. No wrinkles, save those of character about the mouth and the network woven by sun and wind and snow about the fine brown eyes, marked the dark, straight-featured face. The knit sash of woven crimson and yellow and green and white, a sash that is seldom seen outside the Hudson's Bay country, was about the half-breed's slim waist. He must have been sixty years old, yet his movements were smooth and quick as those of youth.

"Maybee," he said in the deep musical voice that came from behind white, even teeth, "you keel dat man. She'll be hell *pour* you, den. Weeth my han's I bust de back. You bettair go."

203

"Ain't that my carbine yuh got?" snarled the unwilling Waldron.

"*Oui*," said the half-breed, smiling widely and nodding.

Sim Waldron, loath as he was to depart, walked to his horse and swung into the saddle. "I ain't in the habit uh takin' Injun orders," he spoke from his horse. "Don't think fer a second that yo're winnin' much."

Whirling his horse, the defeated Sim Waldron, bloody, sick with pain, rode for home.

CHAPTER
SEVEN

John Moss woke to see that the sun rode high in the cloudless sky. He was not lying where he had fallen, but in quite another spot. His own coat had pillowed his head, which now was bathed and bandaged. His own saddle blanket lay under him. His .45s and carbine lay beside him.

He sat up slowly, pains racking his body, his head splitting with aching stabs. He expected to see someone, he knew not who. But, save for the grazing Scarlet, he was alone. Then his eyes fell on a white oblong envelope tucked in a pocket of his buckskin coat. Even before he drew the letter from the pocket, he recognized it. It was Barlow Burkett's sealed letter. There were the red seals holding down the flap. Across its white, now somewhat soiled surface, were the words: **Barlow Burkett. To be opened after his death.** He examined the envelope and seals closely. So far as he could discern, no hand had disturbed the seals. The red blotches of hard wax, stamped with the seal ring of the House of Moss, were intact.

John Moss ached in every nerve and muscle. Recalling the treachery of Sim Waldron, he smiled wryly. The cut behind his ear pained and throbbed as a reminder. Had Sim Waldron struck him down, then bandaged his head and given him the stolen letter? Hardly. That was not Sim Waldron's way. Someone, then, had intervened. That someone was the person who had left the letter. By the same course of reasoning that someone was the man who last night had killed the man who had shot at John Moss through the window. But who was that man? Why had he gone away after leaving the letter? Why had he taken the letter if he had not read it? Where was that man now?

John Moss gave it up. His saddle and bridle lay nearby. Picking up his bridle, he approached Scarlet. A bit of paper was tied to the foretop of the big bay gelding. As Scarlet snorted in mild fright at the blood odor on his master, John Moss read the note:

In God's name, go back!

He had never seen that handwriting. Vertical, round-lettered, childish were those words of frantic warning. John Moss smiled. But one person could have gone close enough to Scarlet to fasten the note to the horse's foretop. That person was White Fawn.

Slowly, every movement one of pain, John Moss saddled and mounted. A grim smile played about his bruised mouth as he rode on.

"Go back?" he muttered inaudibly through swollen lips. "Now? Hardly." Yet as he rode along the silent trail, he felt that eyes followed him and those eyes were not friendly in their scrutiny.

206

The gait of the horse increased the throbbing pain in his head. His tongue was dry inside his mouth. He headed for a water hole five miles away. And when he came to the spot, he received warning of the unseen power that dogged his trail. For the water hole was filled with slimy mud. Fresh shovel marks told their story. Someone had deliberately fouled the water hole. The closest water lay along the back trail about twelve miles. Ahead, ten miles, were some springs. But John Moss knew that the same hands that fouled the water hole would also cover the springs, springs that were but a tiny trickle from a mossy spot in the cedars. Twenty-five miles beyond those springs lay a river.

"Well, they can't fill up a river," he mumbled grimly, and rode on, jaws clamped, eyes red under puffed, discolored lids.

Every mile seemed ten to the pain-racked John Moss but he showed no indication of turning back. He barely glanced at the tiny spring that was now hidden beneath freshly shoveled earth trampled into oozing mud.

He rode on past the buried spring, through the fringe of junipers, headed for the distant river. Scarlet kept on at a steady swinging walk that was as fast as the trot of an ungaited horse. Mile after mile he went, with the sun dropping lower in the west. Shadows grew longer, the hush of the wilderness more sinister with the coming of sunset.

John Moss's head was clearing somewhat of pain now, but every fiber of his body called for water. As the last streak of a setting sun painted the sky, he rode down a rocky slope toward a ribbon of water —

Mormon Creek, so called because once there had been a Mormon colony near its headwaters. The adobe walls of its time-ruined buildings still stood. It was said that a band of cattle rustlers and outlaws used the place as a rendezvous.

John Moss dismounted and slipped Scarlet's bridle off. Then horse and man drank their fill. The nicker of a horse brought both Moss and Scarlet erect, listening.

John Moss, a .45 in his hand, stepped back behind some boulders and waited. Scarlet answered the call of the unseen horse. Scarlet's headstall was back on his neck, the knotted bridle-reins dropped over the saddle horn. Forehoofs in the water, the beautiful bay stood listening, ears pointing, head lifted, nostrils twitching.

From across the stream came the sound of shod hoofs. A man on a rangy, dun-colored horse came into view. The man held a Winchester in the crook of his arm. Under a low-pulled hat, a pair of narrowed eyes stared at Scarlet. The man sat sidewise in his saddle, then pulled a square of plug from a shirt pocket and bit off a corner. To the watching John Moss the fellow was a stranger.

"Come on out, Moss!" called the man on the dun horse, shoving his rifle back in its saddle scabbard. "Nobody's gonna do no shootin'."

"Who are you?" called John Moss, fearing some sort of trap.

"Now that's a kinda puzzlin' question, mister," came the pleasant reply. "I done changed names so many times I clean fergot my real 'un. Yuh kin call me Shorty er somethin' like that. I was on my way tuh camp when

I sights yuh comin' off the ridge. Couldn't make yuh out without field glasses. Seen yuh duck when Buck nickered. Rid down tuh look at yore earmarks. Recognized yore hoss. I didn't have these whiskers the night I laid over at the Ranch of the Four Winds a year ago last October. I'm the short, sandy-complected jasper as played the mouth harp that evenin'. Slim-built boy with me. A sheriff two days behind us. Mind me now?"

John Moss stepped into the open. He remembered this short-statured, whimsical sort of fellow who had, in company with a wounded companion, once sought shelter at his house. The man was an outlaw, a rustler of stolen stock, but John Moss felt no fear of harm as he greeted the fellow, a wizened man with bright blue eyes that puckered into sunny slits when he grinned. The smiling eyes now peered from a graying straw-colored thatch of beard.

"I got whiskers like a Mormon bishop," Shorty announced, "an' I ain't much fer looks, but yo're wuss-lookin', Moss. Whatever kind uh varmint have yuh bin fightin'? Looks like yuh'd bin rasslin' with a lion."

"I had a tie-up with Sim Waldron." Moss gripped the little outlaw's hand in greeting.

"Well, I'll be danged! Sim Waldron, eh? The new sheriff uh Hackberry." Shorty spat as if the name tasted bad in his mouth. "I'd like tuh see what Waldron looks like by now. Kill him?"

John Moss smiled and shook his head. Then he made a dipper of his hat brim and drank thirstily, the little horse thief watching him, something more than amused interest in his puckered blue eyes.

"Us boys is camped at the 'dobe ruins," he voiced a studiedly careless invitation. "Yo're welcome to what we got in the way uh grub."

"I'll just take you up on that," John Moss accepted as he gingerly bathed his battered face.

When he finished washing, John Moss slipped Scarlet's bridle on and followed the little outlaw across the creek and along a dim trail that led to the adobe ruins five miles up the creek.

"Yuh always bin on the square with us fellers," said Shorty as the trail widened to permit their traveling abreast. "If yo're into some sort uh tight, say the word an' we'll take chips in the game. We ain't none of us fond of the Waldrons. Not since Sim glaumed hisse'f a sheriff's star an' begin lawin' boys he's rode with along a crooked trail. He ain't no better than us. Fact is he's ornerier'n us. Fer he wears that tin star tuh cover what crooked deals he kin swing.

"Barlow Burkett's different," the outlaw went on. "Ornery as hell an' proud of it. Wouldn't wear a badge if yuh give him one. He don't claim tuh be nothin' but mean. He's a ol' he-wolf an' says so when he howls. Yet I've knowed that danged rascal tuh do some good turns fer folks. Yuh'd never git him to admit it, though. I usta work fer ol' Barlow . . . good man tuh work fer. Him an' the Injuns was all the same them days. He knowed their language an' kinda half believed their religion."

"It was Barlow Burkett that hid Dyin' Day in the cliff dwellin' at Montezuma Castle when them red-coated

Canadian police come plumb from Canada fer him. Barlow shows 'em a grave an' hands 'em a pick an' shovel. They dug up the bones an' some trinkets which they taken back. I reckon they reported to the boss Red Coat that they'd got their man. They'd uh shore felt cheap if they knowed it was no more ner less than a Waldron that ol' Barlow had killed an' planted as a warnin' fer Lash an' Sim an' their daddy."

Shorty chuckled reminiscently. John Moss, his eyes burning oddly, held his tongue, hoping Shorty would continue.

"Barlow never had no time fer law folks, American, Mex, er Canadian," Shorty continued. "Hated 'em all. Barlow always claimed that Colonel Colt was the only law he respected. Him an' Dyin' Day usta argue of a evenin' about law. Too bad yuh never knowed Dyin' Day. He was afore yore time. But he was a gentleman and knowed about books an' law. I never did know his name. Barlow called him Dyin' Day. Didn't Waldron never tell yuh about him?"

"No," admitted John Moss. "What an odd nickname, Dying Day."

"Then I reckon" — Shorty grinned wisely — "I better quit runnin' off at the head. It never wins a man nothin' but trouble tuh git mouthy."

"Is this Dying Day still living?"

"Shucks, no. Died years ago." There was a note of finality to the outlaw's statement that definitely closed the subject. John Moss knew that he must seek farther than the outlaw camp for that which he wished to know.

From a rocky pinnacle, a pair of dark eyes watched the two white men. The watcher was an Indian, naked save for a breechcloth. When the two riders established a definite course, the Indian left his station and trotted off with a tireless, light-footed gait equal to that of a horse. The Zuñi runner can outdistance a horse where the going is rough. Within a few hours news of John Moss's presence at the outlaw camp at the adobe ruins would reach the ears of those who waited.

CHAPTER
EIGHT

No written record stamps the date of the cliff dwellings. By word of mouth the tale comes down in legend and song. Out of a past long silent and laden with the dust of centuries comes the legendary tale of the Bat People who dwelt there, a tale told by a priest of the Hopi people, a priest so old that he has been blind since even the old men remember, and perhaps the facts have become blended with dreams. Who knows? Under the cliff ledge are houses, inaccessible from below, for the ladders are gone. In these silent places of a vanished people, where dust lies unmarked upon the floor that is centuries old, the voice instinctively drops to an awed undertone. No cathedral could be more sublime in its silence than this abandoned dwelling place of the vanished Bat People. The voices of men gave sound now — puny sound against that mammoth cliff that looks out across endless miles of purpling hills.

"Tell him" — it was Barlow Burkett who spoke to White Fawn, who acted as interpreter for Eagle Chief — "that I have come from the Ranch of the Four Winds, that I have talked to John Moss."

White Fawn interpreted swiftly. The three were seated in a room that showed many traces of being the

213

temporary home of Eagle Chief and his foster daughter. A long rope from the cliff above was the only means of exit or entrance to this dwelling of the Bat People known among white men as Montezuma Castle. The old Sioux listened patiently. He sucked at the long stem of a red clay pipe. Finally he spoke.

"You are a good man, friend. You have the brave heart and the wisdom of white hairs. Eagle Chief reads in the eyes of his friend that John Moss grows restless like the wolf in the cage. Yet the time has not yet come for him to know many things."

White Fawn interpreted the words of the old Sioux. In her heart she wondered what those things were that John Moss was someday to know. The habit of obedience and silence was well learned by this girl who had lived always among the Indians. She saw a frown of annoyance on the brow of Barlow Burkett, who she had seen at irregular intervals during the past years.

"Tell him," said Burkett, measuring his words, "that John Moss has taken up the trail already. He's right set in his ways. He won't turn back till he finds what he's looking for. Tell him that John Moss has a good heart. His tongue does not lie. His house is a house of council, where men sit and smoke. Tell Eagle Chief that."

Again the girl translated. Once more smoke curled from the pipe of red clay. After a long time the old Sioux spoke.

"I am an old man. I have had a dream. Before the moon comes again Eagle Chief will die and his spirit will ride across the shadow hills. Perhaps you, who know the heart of John Moss, speak with much wisdom. It is well that, before I die, I ride to the Ranch of the Four Winds. For three days and nights now, I sit here and smoke. John Moss will know of his father. He shall hear the story of him we called the White Eagle. From my daughter and from Antoine I have learned much of the son of White Eagle. Antoine tells that he is a man of peace. That is good. But before he is told those many things, John Moss, son of White Eagle, must prove that he is a warrior."

With the patience of one accustomed to the deliberate judgment of the Indian, Burkett listened to the translation of the old chief's words.

"How is John Moss to prove he is brave?" he asked through White Fawn.

"I have had a dream," spoke Eagle Chief solemnly. "Many men were fighting with guns. Among those men who fought was John Moss, son of the white chief we called White Eagle."

White Fawn, her eyes dark with pain and fear, translated. The he-wolf of the Burkett feudists, a faint smile on his mouth, eyed the Indian sharply.

"You are friend to John Moss," said White Fawn. "You must save him." Her voice held a tremor of fear. Burkett eyed the girl gravely.

"I'm doing all I can," he said, not unkindly, "but John Moss has a mind of his own."

"He is a brave man. What need is there for him to die to prove he is brave? I do not believe too much in dreams." She would have said more, perhaps, had she not felt the Indian's penetrating gaze reading her thoughts. Even the white-skinned foster daughter of a chief has no voice when men hold council.

The last slanting rays of the sunset passed across the dwelling place of the Bat People. As the short Southwest twilight came, Barlow Burkett climbed the rope to the mesa above and pulled the rope up after him. Thus the means of entrance to the hiding place of Eagle Chief and his foster daughter was gone.

The girl and the old Indian were now alone. Her eyes clouded with foreboding as she prepared their evening meal. Eagle Chief, a lonely, blanket-wrapped figure, sat smoking, his old eyes following the twilight shadows to the skyline beyond. For him, life was almost done and he was content to live his last days in retrospect of a youth filled with danger. But one task remained for him, a task that had to do with John Moss. When that was done, he would chant his death song to Manitou. The spirit would leave his body to ride across the shadow hills where fat meat is plentiful for those who die with bravery in their hearts.

Barlow Burkett rode into the dusk. His old face was set and hard. No peace softened his old age, only bitterness and a vow of vengeance. Men with naked guns roamed the hills, hunting him as if he were a mad beast. They would shoot him down without a chance. There was a reward for Barlow Burkett, dead or alive, a bounty on the white scalp of the he-wolf of the Burketts.

A grim smile crossed his face as he headed for the adobe ruins on Mormon Creek. He rode with his hand near his gun, his cold eyes always alert, a sinister solitary figure.

"*¿Quién es?*" rasped a challenge from a rocky cañnon down which old Burkett rode.

"*Amigo*," called Burkett softly.

"That you, Barlow?"

"Shore is. How's tricks?"

"We got a herd gathered that a man can't shoot acrost."

"Straight Flying-W stuff?"

"Mostly. Too big a gatherment tuh work clean. There's a heap uh your'n with the brands worked into some kinda curious figure." The man rode into the trail now, a carbine across his saddle.

"Ary trouble?"

"Nope. A couple of Waldron hands spotted us and rode off fer home tuh tell Sim his range was being skunked. Sim'll curl up and die uh hate. Bite hisse'f like a rattler, I bet."

Burkett chuckled. "The danged skunk tribe! I'll learn 'em!"

"Shorty brung in a stray . . . John Moss."

"What?"

"Yeah. Moss and Sim locked horns. Moss is kinda beat up. I bet that big feller kin go some when he's riled. Like tuh see what Sim looks like."

Burkett rode on down the cañon. He passed out of the cañon to a wide valley. A huge herd of cattle was being bedded down by half a dozen shadowy riders who were well mounted and heavily armed. Burkett traded a few casual remarks with them, then headed for the spot of distant firelight where camp was pitched.

A group of men lounged about the fire. Horses, saddled and ready for an emergency, were tied to a rope corral. A cook puttered about his Dutch ovens. It might have been a lawful roundup camp save for the array of guns and the alert vigilance thinly hidden behind the careless fireside banter.

Among these men squatted John Moss, a pipe in his mouth. He had seen that stolen herd and knew that he had stumbled onto some grim deviltry. He showed little surprise when Barlow Burkett rode up out of the new night.

Burkett nodded to the group, pulling off his gloves and holding stiff hands to the blaze as he squatted beside Moss.

"Getting chilly these nights, or my ol' blood's a-thinning. Ain't you kind of strayed some, John Moss?"

"Didn't know I was horning into a game, Burkett. If I'm intruding, speak up."

"Don't see any need of yore pulling out tonight. Don't really look for bad trouble till we get outta the Mogollons. I'm skinning the Waldrons for keeps. Trailing into old Mexico with this stuff. It's gonna be a big drive."

"Supposing the Waldron outfit stops the drive?"

A slow, grim smile spread Barlow Burkett's mouth. He rolled and lit a cigarette before he spoke. His eyes were hard and cruel as they stared broodingly into the firelight.

"That'll be to their sorrow," he said.

218

CHAPTER
NINE

A lanky man in patched chaps played wheezy tunes on a harmonica. Others talked aimlessly. The cook fussed over his pots, whistling tunelessly. From the shadows came the crunching of grazing horses. Above them glittered the white stars in a cloudless, chilly night.

Hard-eyed men they were, who rode dim trails, just beyond the long reach of the law — rustlers, killers, men who placed small value on life, be it their own or the life of an enemy. To a man they would someday pay the price of their crimes. Until that day came, they would ride along their way.

Law was a primitive, crude weapon in that country. There were men in the offices of sheriff, marshal, and deputy who were little better than outlaws. The cattle barons had hired killers on their payrolls. Men with a price on their heads were absolved of their crimes and made law officers by a desperate, harassed country seeking protection from the outlaw element. For this was the heyday of men like Billy the Kid, the Earp gang, the Horrel boys, when New Mexico and Arizona were drenched with blood, when Tombstone and Dodge and Santa Fe were cities in swift transition. There was but a thin line that shrank at times to invisibility, separating law from lawless. The swift crash of an ex-outlaw's gun was to bring law to Tombstone. In Lincoln County, across the New Mexico line, the McSween and Murphy factions were trading hot bullets.

From this drenching of blood would spring law. The cattle wars would become history. A new regime would swing into harness. It was a period of change, during which the killers were doing their own weeding out. Soon there would be no market for stolen herds. But just now the killers' guns were harvesting stolen crops. A man was as good as his speed with a gun, no better.

No qualm of conscience marred John Moss's evening among this gathering. He knew that Sim Waldron, sheriff of Hackberry, was worse than any among them. He neither upheld this company nor did he condemn their lights. He ate their food, listened to their talk, shared his tobacco with them, and he found it difficult to condemn them for being what they were. Because they understood his attitude, they accepted his presence.

He was listening to one of them who had recently come from Dodge City. The man was lauding the merits and courage of Bat Masterson, the new sheriff.

"There," he announced with conviction, "is a *man!*"

Another spoke of John Slaughter, the cattleman who now enforced the law at Tombstone, another fearless man who was bringing law out of powder smoke. It was a conversation to hold the interest of any man. John Moss listened raptly to the doings of that youngster

220

whose guns were belching death over in New Mexico —William Bonney, better known as Billy the Kid.

And finally, when John Moss turned to engage Barlow Burkett in the subject that now so vitally concerned him, Burkett was gone. He had slipped from the circle and vanished. Nor was he to be found out at the herd. The wily old he-wolf was prowling somewhere, watching, listening, wary. Second guard had ridden out to the herd when John Moss returned to the campfire. Besides the graying coals squatted a slight figure. Save for that solitary figure, the others slept. In the dim light, John Moss did not recognize the lone watcher. When he did, he gave a short gasp of surprise. For the figure by the dead fire was that of White Fawn.

She motioned him to silence and he followed her into the night. Their moccasins made no sound. Presently they stood side-by-side, a hundred yards from the camp. Through every fiber of his body emotion swept John Moss. He wanted more than anything in the world to take this strange girl in his arms and keep her there for always. Yet he could not. He *must* not. There was that ring that had been her father's ring, the ring with the coat of arms of Moss. Could this girl be his half-sister?

"Why do you come here?" he asked, holding her hands tightly and looking down into her eyes.

"To save you," she said. "You must go back home. Something terrible is going to happen. The Indians know. Barlow Burkett knows. There is more than foolish medicine dreams that makes Eagle Chief talk so of dead men. Tonight, when Antoine returned, he told

221

of a man dead at the Ranch of the Four Winds. And never, never shall I forget that fight I watched, when you and that man fought like dogs over a bone. Antoine kept me from screaming. Then he saved that man from killing you with a gun when you lay so quiet I thought you dead. I tied a note to your horse. Why did you still come?"

"To find you," he replied huskily, "to find you and Eagle Chief and this Antoine fellow, to learn the truth about my father and about you. That ring you wear was my father's ring. If he was also your father, you are my sister."

He felt her hands tighten in his clasp. "I do not think you are my brother." Her voice was but a faint whisper.

"But you say this ring was your father's?"

"It was given to my father. After I had seen that same coat of arms above your fireplace, I made Antoine tell me."

"You were at my house? When?"

"That night I ran away from you at your camp. I looked in the window. Barlow Burkett sat there by the fire. I saw the shield above the fireplace. So I rode home and made Antoine tell me why my ring and the shield of John Moss are the same. But he would not tell me much."

"What did he say?"

"He said that your father gave my father that ring."

"Then you can't be my sister."

"No."

Without a word, John Moss took her in his arms. A tired little sob sighed from her lips as she felt the protecting comfort of his arms. "I love you," he said softly. "I've loved you since that day you saved my life five years ago. You aren't afraid of me?"

"Should I be afraid of the man I love?" She laughed happily. "Now you will go back to the Ranch of the Four Winds?"

"When I have seen Eagle Chief, your foster father. I'm going to learn about my father and your father, who you are and why you were hidden here."

"I am afraid for you. What does it matter, now, what happened so long ago? I will go with you to your home and stay there always. It will be a house of peace where men sit and smoke, where white man and Indian blow smoke to the four winds. I am afraid for you. Always, when Eagle Chief has a dream, that dream happens. Now he has dreamed of dead men, of men fighting with guns and you among them. That is why I came away. Not even Antoine knows of the hidden trail that leads down the cliff from the home of the Bat People."

"That's where you hide from me, eh?" John Moss smiled, holding her in his arms and looking into her troubled eyes. "Montezuma's Castle, eh?"

"You must never come there. Promise me that. If you love me, make me that promise. For Eagle Chief would know I had told and would punish me."

"Beat you?"

"Oh, no. He never hurts me. But he would make me stay home. He would keep me there and take away my books. He is never cruel. Only he is very proud. He wants you to be a warrior as well as a man of council.

He is a Sioux and that is the way of his people. He is a fine man."

"I understand. I won't force my way to your home. But tonight I'll ride back with you to the foot of the cliff."

"That will be nice." She laughed gently as they got their horses.

Past the herd and its singing riders, John Moss paused to identify himself and the girl.

"Fine evenin' fer a ride." Shorty grinned. "Yo're a lucky cuss, Moss. But be careful some Waldrons don't sight yuh."

Across the rough hills, along the moonlit mesa, John Moss and White Fawn rode with stirrups touching. He could not remember when he had been so happy. Yet always he kept a wary eye open for riders of the night.

White Fawn was utterly blissful. This man was her lover, her god, her very life. She asked nothing more of life than to be always with him.

Ahead, perhaps half a mile distant, rose the sheer wall of the Bat People. Here they halted, for they deemed it unwise for John Moss to risk being seen by the vigilant Antoine. Some light love message suddenly died unspoken on John Moss's lips.

"Quick," he whispered in her ear, leading the horses into some brush. "Someone's coming."

The kind hand of chance had led the two lovers from the main trail. They were well hidden in the dense brush. From this vantage point they saw a string of riders pass single file along the main trail that led to the outlaw camp on Mormon Creek. One of the riders lit a match and held the cupped flame to his cigarette. For a moment the smoker's battered face was revealed to the watchers. The man was Sim Waldron. John Moss counted twenty-five men in the posse that rode in wordless silence, their saddles creaking and shod hoofs clicking, with the moonlight falling on their naked gun barrels.

"Now, dear," whispered John Moss, when the last rider had gone from view, "I'll have to hurry back to camp. Barlow Burkett is my friend and I'm not going to let these night-prowling devils catch him unawares. Promise me not to leave home until I send for you. This country is in the climax of an upheaval. Best lay low till the smoke clears."

"It has come true," said the girl huskily, "that dream of Eagle Chief's. Many men fighting. You will be among them. Yet I would not have the man I love be a coward. Kiss me now. Then ride fast. May Manitou make strong your muscles. May he ride with you so that no bullet can harm you. May he send you back to White Fawn. God keep you, John. God, our white man's God, keep you from harm."

So she left him. And so John Moss, man of peace, whose home was the Ranch of the Four Winds, was drawn into that bloody war that swept Mormon Creek from headwaters to where its waters met the Verde. But before the bloody tentacles of that range war reached out to pull him into the horror of that cattle war, John Moss was to make one vain, yet idiotically glorious attempt to halt the impending slaughter. He did not know that the first blood of the Mormon Creek war had already been spilled, that its red taint fouled the threshold of the Ranch of the Four Winds, and that the faithful old squaw lay huddled in the open doorway, her body fairly riddled with bullets.

They had expected to find John Moss there. As they swept down on the house like the rush of a tornado out of a deathly calm, the door had opened. The old Indian woman had stood there in the lit doorway, stolidly puzzled at their coming. Then she had sagged down in her moccasin tracks, more than a score of bullets in her heavy body. Sim Waldron and his men had ransacked the house, splintering furniture, smearing immaculate walls and floors with tobacco juice, leaving in their wake a wreckage of books and overturned chairs and broken crockery and china. Sim Waldron had emptied his six-shooter into the bronze shield above the mantle.

"We'll burn the whole place on the way back. The damned dude!"

They had ridden on into the night in single file, silent of voice, their guns unsheathed, with Sim Waldron's sheriff star glittering mockingly in the moonlight. It was Sim Waldron and his men that John Moss and White Fawn had watched from where they were hidden.

CHAPTER
TEN

John Moss pushed Scarlet to a run. By taking a short cut, he arrived at a spot along the trail where it dropped into a cañon, some minutes ahead of the Waldron night riders. Ripping off part of his undershirt, he fastened the white cloth to a stick and planted the flag of truce near a hastily kindled fire in the middle of the trail. He cached Scarlet up on the side of the steep ridge, then crept back to take a hidden position in the boulders above the trail.

Sim Waldron and his riders saw the blaze and, beyond the little fire, the flag of truce. He halted his men, cursing in a muttered undertone.

"Keerful, buys. It's a Burkett trap." He cocked his Winchester and called out in a loud voice. "Givin' up, Burkett?"

"This is John Moss."

"Now ain't that nice," sneered Sim Waldron. "I got a warrant fer yuh, Moss. One fer Burkett, too. An' the law of Arizona backs my play. Will you give up peaceable er do we drag in yore carcass on the end of a rope?"

"Neither, Sim Waldron. I've broken no laws. I'm warning you to go back where you came from. Burkett is ready for you. He'll fight to the end. You may get him but he and his men will die fighting. This is not Arizona law you are enforcing. It's Waldron law. You know it. Your men know it. If you and Barlow Burkett will come to my house, you will get a fair hearing."

"Dry up, yuh damned Johnny Bull. You ain't even a citizen. You and yore Injun ways don't set good with us folks. We're cleanin' the range uh squawmen. We'll hang yuh an' the old he-wolf Burkett side-by-side. Yuh horned in where yuh had no business. Yuh murdered Lash. Yuh killed one uh my men that come tuh yore place peaceful. Yo're gonna pay fer them two lives. Git the damned tenderfoot, boys!"

Sim Waldron emptied his gun at the spot whence John Moss's voice had come. His men followed suit. The cañon rang with the crashing echoes of gunfire. Then, at a signal, they ceased firing. It seemed impossible that Moss could have remained unscathed in that hail of lead.

"Got aplenty?" called Sim Waldron when the echoes of the shots died away.

A laugh floated down from the side of the cañon. It was not a pleasant-sounding laugh. There can be little humor in mirth that comes through powder smoke.

"You've saved me a ride, Waldron. The sound of those shots will warn Burkett and his men. For a man in your position, you're an awful ass, my dear fellow. I could pick you off where you sit your horse, if I were a murdering breed. But Burkett will want that honor, so I'm letting you ride on. They'll be ready for you when you get there. If your men have the sense of two-year-olds, they'll turn back. I may add, my murdering friend, that your shots have not touched me. Quite a waste of bullets."

The derisive tone of the hidden John Moss angered Sim Waldron to a further outburst. "We got yore damn' squaw, Moss. We'd uh got yuh, only yuh was scared tuh go home. Yore purty Injun rugs is kinda mussed up. We're burnin' that snake nest on our way home. Come on, boys, let's git goin'. If yuh sight Moss, kill 'im. Keep yore eyes peeled."

With a nasty laugh, Sim Waldron lifted his gun, took quick aim at the stick that held the white flag, and pressed the trigger. The bullet severed the stick. Waldron's men rode over the trampled symbol of peace.

John Moss climbed cautiously up the slope to where he had left Scarlet. Taking a trail known to few white men, he rode for the camp at the adobe ruins.

It was almost half an hour later that a voice barked harsh challenge.

"*¿Quién es?*"

"*Amigo*, John Moss. That you, Shorty?"

"That's me, pardner. Yo're back quick, considerin'."

"Sim Waldron's riding this way with twenty-five men. Didn't you boys hear the shooting?"

"We heerd somethin' odd but it was a long ways off. Twenty-five of 'em, eh? About two apiece fer us fellers. I'll git word to the boys on herd if yuh'll ride down tuh camp an' tell Barlow. Sim ain't wastin' no time."

At camp John Moss told Burkett of the Waldron approach. The old feudist chuckled grimly.

"He thinks I got only three, four men. He'll get a dose he ain't expecting. Did Antoine find you and the gal?"

229

"No. Who is Antoine, anyhow?"

"You'll find out when I'm dead, son. Mebby you'll find out before I'm gone. Dunno. Him and that Sioux Eagle Chief are moving to your place tonight. Antoine knew White Fawn came here, so he followed. She's to go with 'em to the Ranch of the Four Winds. The old Injun's about ready to make medicine talk. It's about time, too. Injuns are slow that-a-way. I reckon Antoine talked turkey to him. Now that you and the gal have met, you'd bust hell open learning things. Antoine must've put a bug in his ear. Well, I gotta be going. If I don't see you no more, so long. Keep outta this fighting, John Moss. You've got a woman to care for now. She's a good gal. You're a good man. I'm wishin' you both happiness."

The old he-wolf shoved out a hand and John Moss took it.

"Be good to the gal, John. She's had a tough life. Take her outta this country. Take her home, Sir John Moss. Neither of you fit in with this country. Ride like hell outta this. It ain't your fight. Antoine and Eagle Chief and the gal'll be at the Ranch of the Four Winds when you get there, like as not. So long!"

Old Barlow Burkett gave John Moss's hand a parting grip, then called his men to action. Even the cook swung into a saddle, a long-barreled rifle in his hand. With a careless — "*Adiós*, Moss!" — they faded into the night. John Moss was alone beside the dead fire. In the east, the first thin streak of a red dawn showed in the sky. It was the dawn of a day of bloodshed, the

230

beginning of the battle that was to go down in the history of the Southwest as the Mormon Creek War.

John Moss swung Scarlet to a long lope. He was following the advice of the old he-wolf. He was headed for home. Nor was he at all sure but what the Waldrons would be there ahead of him. Sim Waldron had made the boast that they had killed the old squaw. Perhaps Sim had lied, but most probably the man had spoken the truth. Slow rage took possession of him as he pictured that invasion of his home. If they had murdered the faithful old squaw, they must pay the full penalty.

Behind him came the sound of firing. The war was on. Then he heard the bawling of confused cattle. The Waldrons had stampeded the big herd.

Three riders tore at a run up out of a long draw, swift-moving gray blots in the half light of the dawn that was shot with crimson. They came in from an angle, leading in the same direction in which John Moss traveled.

The Briton gripped his carbine and touched Scarlet with unspurred heels. The big bay, as if this were the sport he loved, leaped forward, rapidly gaining on the three riders. Two of them kept on at top speed, lying low along their horses' necks. The third slackened his pace, as if waiting to do battle. Then, from the long draw, four more riders shot into view, riding hard.

As these four men headed for the trail apparently to cut off the first three riders, John Moss recognized two of them as Waldron men. The other three, the ones pursued, must then be Burkett men. It was hard to recognize them in the bad light. Without checking the gait of his horse, John Moss stood in his stirrups and took a snap shot at the foremost of the four Waldron men. The shot came close. The four men now saw him for the first time. Their bullets whined around him.

That other rider from the first group now whirled his horse and rode for the four men pointblank. The crimson flash of his gun streaked rapidly. Then, as he came within range, he veered off, heading toward Moss. As he dropped a Waldron man, he yelled. There was no mistaking that yell. It was the war cry of the Cree. Eagle Chief? Antoine? It must be one of the two. John Moss wondered if the man recognized him. There was little time for speculation. He rode at a run, shooting, reloading. He dropped one of the Waldron men. The two remaining men whirled their horses and rode back into the draw.

One of their number lay in a motionless heap. The other one crawled for shelter. John Moss rode toward the man who had given the Cree war cry. As he came close, he held up his arm in the sign of peace. The rider did likewise.

"By gar," boomed a big voice, as John Moss came up, "dem feller she'll fight lak' hell *pour* leetle tam. Den, when de odds she's even, dey ron. Ho, my good frien', John Moss. Me, I'm Antoine, de stronges' dam' man in Quebec. *Bo' jou', m'sieu.*"

The white-maned half-breed grinned and shoved out a hand. John Moss took it heartily. There was something fascinating about the man's smile.

232

"Me, I'm see you come 'cross de heel. I'm say to old man . . . 'She's our good frien', John Moss.' Old man, she's shake de head. De eyes *pour* de old man ain't so good. But me, Antoine, I'm know dat red horse. Damn' lucky, eh?"

"White Fawn and Eagle Chief?" asked John Moss. Antoine pointed to the two riders ahead.

"I'm tell dem to ride along. Bimeby, when I'm keel t'ree, four fellers, I'm catch up."

"I had an idea that you were a younger man," said John Moss as they rode along together, hastening to overtake the old Indian and the girl.

"No, jus' old man, *m'sieu*. Old enough to be dat White Fawn's papa." His deep chuckle followed John Moss's sudden blush. "Me, I'm onderstan' 'bout dem things."

The firing behind them had almost died away in the distance. The sun was rising when they caught up with White Fawn and Eagle Chief. The girl's smile was as glorious as the sunrise. The old Sioux shook hands gravely, his dark eyes appraising the white man. Whatever was the result of that careful appraisal, it was hidden behind the masklike face of the old warrior.

They rode on at a stiff trot. At a covert signal from Antoine, John Moss dropped back with him.

With dramatic brevity Antoine told him that the squaw at the Ranch of the Four Winds had been killed. A Hopi runner had brought word. Her people had taken away her body for burial. If only these people of hers were the Cree or the Blackfeet or the Assiniboine, there would be a fight. But these were the people of peace, with their pottery and blanket-making and farming.

"She's bad *pour* dem fellers to shoot the Hopi woman lak' dat. You bet my life, my good frien', eh?"

John Moss nodded. These southern tribes lacked the war-like temperament of the northern tribes. Save for the wily and cruel Apaches the Southwest Indians were men of peace.

"Dat old woman, she's fight, too. Dat night when one feller shoot de window, she keel dat man."

"What's that?"

"You bet. Me, I'm camp nearby. I'm hear dat shot. I'm come queeck. But de man, she's dead 'hind de woodshed. Old squaw, he's tell me 'bout keel dat feller weeth de knife. Den dat squaw take de letter weeth de red seal. He's geeve dat letter to me. Maybe planty money in de letter. Dem fellers keel you *pour* dat money, so old squaw steal de money and geeve to Antoine to keep safe *pour* you. I'm put dat letter in your pocket dat tam you mak' de fight weeth dat Waldron. Mebbyso Sim Waldron, she's know dat old squaw keel dat man, eh?"

"Perhaps." John Moss was tangled in a hundred thoughts. The mystery of the stolen letter was explained now. He wanted to ask Antoine more questions but he knew the time had not come for that. That old squaw had saved his life and probably been murdered because of that loyalty to her white employer. Something told John Moss that there was to be more bloodshed before Sim Waldron finished, that the Ranch of the Four

Winds was to become a house of battle rather than of peace.

Old Eagle Chief, riding ahead, his back as straight as a warrior's lance, scanned the country about them with slitted black eyes. His face and hair were streaked with red war paint. His blanket had slipped from his shoulders, leaving a naked torso, the arms and chest heavily marked with scars of youthful sun dances when the braves tortured themselves. A cruel twist was on his wide mouth. As he rode, he chanted the war song of his people. A single eagle feather was braided into his scalp lock. There was an ugly-looking knife in a beaded sheath. He carried bow and arrows besides a long-barreled, black-powder .45–70 in the crook of his arm. A strange figure in a strange land, this old Sioux warrior who chanted past deeds in a guttural monotone, his medicine dream was coming to pass. He was ready. He asked no more of his Manitou than a brave death.

Behind him rode the white girl in her beaded clothes and blanket. John Moss and Antoine brought up the rear, wary eyes searching every thicket and clump of rocks for an enemy.

An odd-appearing quartet, indeed, were they who now rode up to the rock house on Desolation Mesa. They put up their horses and went into the house. Dark stains on the threshold marked the passing of the faithful squaw of the Hopi people. Inside was the wreckage of the marauders.

Old Eagle Chief pointed to the bullet-scarred shield above the mantelpiece. While he spoke no word, his old

235

face lighted with emotion. His hands moved swiftly in sign language:

"I am Eagle Chief, friend of White Eagle who rides the valleys of the shadow hills. I have come to this lodge of White Eagle's son. I have kept my word. In the Lodge of the Four Winds I shall die. My heart is glad. I am an old man and I am ready. I am not afraid."

Throughout the day, while Antoine and John Moss kept watch, the old Sioux squatted on the floor in front of the fireplace, smoking and talking to himself. Sometimes the undertone of a song came from his lips. Eagle Chief was preparing to die.

"Gives a man the creeps," the Briton told the girl.

"I have never seen him like this. He is very sad but very happy, also. He had a dream that told him he would die."

They sat together in a window seat. Antoine kept watch from the stable. The shadows of evening were creeping across the hills. Heavy shutters now covered the windows; an ominous silence hung like a pall over the place. The girl prepared the meals and straightened up the house. Filled with restless foreboding, Antoine and John Moss stood guard. Only Eagle Chief seemed calm — calm with that fatalism that told him of the nearness of death.

With dusk came a Hopi runner. He had come from Mormon Creek. He said that the white men had been fighting all day, that some had died. The cattle had been run off and scattered. Barlow Burkett was unhurt and fighting like ten men, shooting, riding recklessly here and there, calling bitter taunts to Sim Waldron to stand in the open and fight it out man to man. But Sim Waldron was not fighting in the open. He stayed hidden in the rocks.

John Moss said: "If Waldron wins, he and his men will come this way. That's almost a certainty. Even if he retreats, he may pay us a swift visit. Well, we're ready."

The Hopi said that his people were watching day and night. They would give the alarm in time. Those at the Ranch of the Four Winds would not be caught unawares.

"That is good," said John Moss, but did not relax his vigilance.

That night, after they had eaten, Eagle Chief called White Fawn, John Moss, and Antoine. He handed the white man a leather-bound ledger. On its cover was the printed title, done on the weather-worn cover in India ink:

Edward Moss and Dion O'Day
Free Traders
Their diary

CHAPTER
ELEVEN

"Dion O'Day," gasped John Moss. For the name of that gallant Irish gentleman was one that conjured up strange tales of heroism — Sir Dion O'Day, soldier, historian, explorer who had spent an immense fortune somehow and in the end had vanished. Now the name of Dion O'Day was written in ink upon this odd old ledger, together with the name of Edward Moss. "Dion O'Day." John Moss saw Antoine nod and smile. Even the face of the old Sioux lost a trace of its austerity.

"Silver Fox, de Injun call Dion O'Day. She'd be de papa *pour* White Fawn. *Comprenez?* When de mothair die, White Fawn he's purty small. Eagle Chief's old woman, he's tak' care de baby. Injun she don' call de baby de white man's name, Kathleen Mavourneen O'Day. No, by gar. She's call de baby White Fawn."

"Then," said John Moss, smiling oddly at the girl, "your father was Dion O'Day, as gallant, as fearless, and as foolish as even an Irishman can be. He tweaked the combined nose of British Parliament one day over the Irish question. But his speeches are on record as the greatest bits of oratory ever heard. I recall hearing my father say that Dion O'Day was born a hundred years too soon. Ireland was not yet ready for him. My father had been in India and Africa with Colonel O'Day. After one particular fiery oration, Dion O'Day was given the Queen's commission to head an exploration party into the heart of Africa. It was the only way to halt the man in his mad attempt to free Ireland. He stayed in Africa two years. Another year was spent in chronicling the findings of that great expedition that took toll of several brave lives and severely taxed the health of the leader.

"As a mere lad, I recall the memory of Dion O'Day's marriage to Kathleen Mavourneen Moore, reputed to be the most beautiful girl in the British Isles, the belle of the Queen's Court. They went to Canada. Colonel O'Day was given a handsome position in the Dominion. For a time, England heard no more of the firebrand O'Day. Then came the startling news that he had resigned his commission, renounced his title, and was seeking to organize a fur-trading company in opposition to the Hudson's Bay Company.

"My mother had died. I was at Eton when my father was sent to Canada on some mission. As near as I could ever learn, he had been sent there to investigate and, if necessary, blot out the fur company of Dion O'Day. For O'Day's free traders were raising hob with the Hudson's Bay fur trade. The Indians were becoming unfriendly to the British trade and were selling their furs to O'Day's company, whose main trading post lay on the American side of the border.

"I never saw my father after he left England. His letters came regularly, a father's letters to his son. Then the letters became less frequent. Two years later they ceased. I was then told that my father was a traitor to his flag. Not only had he failed, but he had joined an outlawed company of men who sought to despoil the British fur trade. He had left me a comfortable income.

"When the Bar Sinister of treachery was stamped across the coat of arms of Moss, I left school and came to Canada to seek the truth. To all my questions came the same reply. My father was a traitor to his country. Beyond that, I learned nothing. I never learned the details, the facts, or even the barest outline of his life in the Dominion. They said he was dead. He had failed in accomplishing that which he had been sent to do. They told me that Dion O'Day was also dead."

"*Oui*." Antoine nodded vehemently. "By gar, dey lie to you, *m'sieu*. I, Antoine Fiant, who was very good frien' to Moss and Dion O'Day, know dat factor at the Hudson's Bay Pos' mak' de lie. *Oui*. Dose two men, she's plenty alive."

"Yes," agreed John Moss grimly, "they lied. A stranger at Quebec handed me a letter from my father. That letter had come without postmark from the Slave Lake country. It was not signed but I knew the writing. It warned me to go back, that I would be killed if I followed that long trail into the wilderness. But I did not go back. I was determined to find my father and hear the truth from him. I loved my father. I honored him above every man. I would not believe that he was a knave. No more than I ever believed that Dion O'Day had gone stark mad in the Slave Lake country and had become a cannibal. Aye, Antoine, that's the report that got to England . . . that Dion O'Day was living with the

Indians and had gone mad, that they had found him eating human flesh."

"Oh!" The daughter of O'Day gave a sharp cry of horror. In his recital, John Moss had momentarily forgotten what effect those words might have upon her. Engrossed in his subject, he had overlooked her as a factor in this grim tale. Swiftly he took her in his arms.

"Dem fellers lie 'bout dat," growled Antoine. "Me, Antoine, was always weeth dem. Sometimes, when somebody rob de cache, we get hongry. One tam we eat de moccasin an' de dog. Edward Moss an' Dion O'Day an' me. Look!" Antoine took the big ledger and opened it at a marked page. "Read!"

Christmas Day, *John Moss read aloud*. We have been out of food for five days. Last night we finished the last shreds of dog meat. We are forced to proceed without sleds, for we have become too weak to drag even a small load. Sir Edward is snow-blind and delirious from pain and lack of nourishment. Antoine, our guide, is a man of courage and withal a gentleman. I caught him dividing his small share of dog flesh between myself and Sir Edward.

If this be the end, then I shall die in excellent company and happy in the knowledge that my companions are the bravest men I have ever known. So sure as the sun exists, men employed by the British Government have robbed our caches of food. I do not call Great Britain our murderer, but I do say, in all the sanity and sincerity of a man

241

about to die, that employees of the fur company are going beyond their orders in so punishing us. Four times we have been ambushed and were forced to kill men. Two of the men we shot were renegade Americans, murderers thinly disguised as trappers. The third man wore the uniform of a corporal of the Canadian Mounted. Antoine recognizes him, however, as an escaped convict.

May He Whose birthday is Christmas protect my baby girl, the tiny child whose mother is in heaven, dead because of the persecution suffered at the hands of men whose sole purpose in life seems to be the lust for money. My baby is in safe hands, among people who place honour before all things. They will care for her.

Our hope of success in forming a fur company, which will deal fairly with both white and Indian trappers, seems lost. Their furs have been stolen, their supplies robbed, and, in several instances, those free trappers have been mysteriously killed. Would to God the Queen might know of this! I repeat it. It is a handful of men devoid of all honour who are committing these crimes. Their reports are taken as the truth. The real conditions and facts are hidden. We, who have given our fortunes and stand now on the verge of sacrificing our lives in a cause of humanity, are branded at home as outlaws and men of dishonour.

In closing this Christmas Day's chronicle, I repeat that I have never known such courage, generosity, and loyalty in the hearts of men as I have found in Sir Edward Moss and Antoine Fiant.

In the silence that followed the last words, big Antoine stood forth with glistening eyes and features twisted with grief.

"Sir Dion O'Day, she's de braves' of all, *m'sieu.* *Sacre*, what a man!"

Bit by bit, John Moss gathered the history of the free traders. It was a history of Utopian dreams that became heart-broken disillusionment, the courageous fight of two men against a power too great to be changed, the sacrifice of fortunes, happiness, and health, and in the end the supreme sacrifice of the lives of two men in a vain attempt to establish a fur trade that would be just and fair to the trappers.

Sir Edward Moss, sent to suppress Dion O'Day's activities, had joined his old soldier comrade of India and Africa. Together they had fought and starved and suffered. Sir Edward had died there in the far North. The brave Briton sought to save his only son a like fate.

After Sir Edward's death, Antoine and Dion O'Day had left Canada. O'Day was blind. His health had broken. The faithful Antoine had cared for him and had, in the end, taken him to Arizona.

Even there, the long arm of British law had reached for the man's life. The wit of Barlow Burkett, feudist and cowman, had frustrated that attempt. The Red Coats had returned content with the report that Dion O'Day was dead. The Indians had cared for the girl child. They had kept faith with Dion O'Day, the Silver

243

Fox. Because the ravages of scurvy and starvation and smallpox had so horribly disfigured the once handsome face and body of the now sightless Dion O'Day, he had never permitted the child to see him. He had died finally, a pitiful, shambling, sightless cripple.

It was late that night when John Moss finished reading the diary of the two adventurers. Antoine stood by the fire, tears in his eyes. Eagle Chief squatted by the open fire, wrapped in his blanket, smoking, listening to the words of John Moss, who read aloud from the ledger.

The girl sat curled in a blanket beside John Moss on the big couch. She smiled at him through a mist of tears as he closed the big book — the book that told the bitter history of their fathers, the record of heroism in the cause of humanity. And, at the end of its chronicle, he read the final hopes of those two men:

God grant that someday the boy, John, shall meet and love and marry the girl, Kathleen. It was Edward's wish. It is also mine. I trust that they shall be kept in ignorance of this book until they have found each other and are betrothed. Then they shall read the pages of this book and know that God, in His great understanding, places no Bar Sinister upon the crests of Moss or O'Day.

If John be a man, he will follow here. He will be brave and true of heart and tolerant. He shall find the girl, Kathleen, pure of heart and worthy of a real man's love. They shall have the blessing of those two men who were their fathers. God will bless their unity.

Eagle Chief rose. John Moss and Kathleen stood before the old Indian. Solemnly Eagle Chief took their hands and joined them. His old face beamed in myriad wrinkles. Happiness shone in his old eyes.

"Jus' lak' de pries'." Antoine laughed. "By gar, everybody she's happy! *Oui!*"

For the moment they all forgot the danger that threatened. Stark reminder of that black hand of death now shattered their joy — the rush of horses' hoofs outside, the quick rattle of shots, the frantic cry of a wounded man at the door.

His gun gripped tightly, John Moss went to answer the pounding outside the barred door.

CHAPTER
TWELVE

"Open," groaned the voice outside. Bullets spatted the rock house like hissing, pelting hail. The man's voice was frantic. "For God's sake, Moss . . ." The voice slid to a thin moan. John Moss, Antoine close behind him, lifted the heavy bar and pulled open the door.

A streak of fire shot out, searing the Briton's eyes. The burn of powder bit his face as a bullet clipped his cheek. Behind him, big Antoine's bulk moved with incredible swiftness. The half-breed struck, something long and sharp and shiny in his hand.

John Moss, blinded, stunned by the flash of guns that spat out of the shadows, now knew that he had been tricked. There had been no wounded man. He shot from the hip, thumbing the hammer of his Colt, shoulder to shoulder with Antoine, who jerked the lever of a Winchester. Men swarmed out of the dark, charging the open doorway, guns spewing flame. Then Antoine's big bulk heaved the door shut across a threshold where two men writhed in their death agonies.

John Moss shot the heavy iron bar back into place across the closed door. Antoine stood cursing in

French-Cree at a bullet-ripped shoulder. Save for the nicked cheek, John Moss was unhurt.

"That was a fool's trick of mine, opening the door."

"*Oui.*" Antoine grinned. "*Sacre*, she's hot fight *pour* one, two, t'ree seconds, eh, my frien'?"

"Let's get that shoulder fixed," grunted the white man, his eyes searching for Kathleen and finding the girl unharmed. "Jove, where's Eagle Chief?"

Kathleen pointed to the door that led outside from the dead squaw's room. "He told me to let him out, then lock the door again."

"*Oui.*" Antoine nodded calmly. "Old man, she's gone to mak' de beeg fight. She don' onderstan' 'bout fight in de house. T'ree day and t'ree nights dat old man mak' de medicine *pour* beeg fight. Planty smoke, planty sing all 'bout den days when Eagle Chief, she's de strong man, de beeg brave. She sit by de fire all night. She look up at de star' and nam' de star *pour* one enemy. Bi'm'by, if de Sioux medicine, she's good and strong, de star she fall down oot de sky. *Très bien, comprenez?* Dat enemy, she's gonna die *pour* sure lak' hell. *Oui.* Dat old man, she's gon' 'bout now to mak' beeg fight. Lift de hair from de scalp. By gar, she'll do it, too."

"But he left his gun here," said John Moss.

"*Oui.* De gon, she's no good *pour* dat kind of fight. Old man, she'll crawl on de belly lak' de snake. White man, she don' hear dat Injun. She don' see nobody. Den dat old man jomp dam' queeck. De knife she go *kerplunk!* White man, she'll die queeck and old Injun lift de hair."

Even now, Eagle Chief was stalking his enemies, silent, crafty, blending unseen into the black shadows, striking with the silent speed of a cougar, scalping his victims. John Moss shivered a little. He and Kathleen bandaged Antoine's injury, which fortunately was but a flesh wound, messy but not dangerous. The rock house with its heavy shutters made an excellent fort. They had water and food to withstand indefinite siege. The soft-nosed Waldron bullets thudded flatly against the stone walls or buried themselves in the thick shutters. The attacking party would ride away with the coming of dawn.

No light, save the red glow of the dying fire, showed in the large living room. Antoine and John Moss moved about silently on moccasined feet, firing from ingeniously made portholes. The firing out there in the open was half-hearted.

The sudden rush of running horses passed the house. John Moss, from a hidden porthole, saw four loose horses rush past, fright speeding their passage. Scarlet, mane and tail flying, led the other three that the watcher recognized as belonging to his three companions.

"Old man do dat," explained Antoine. "Dem fellers can't steal dem ponies now."

John Moss nodded his understanding. They could not use the horses. Nor could they get to the stable to feed and water the tied animals. Loose, they would not stray far, for Scarlet would remain near the place. It was the way of an Indian to think of the horses.

Time dragged slowly. The firing lulled to spasmodic bursts at long intervals. From out in the night, the yapping of a coyote lifted and died. Antoine chuckled. He whispered in an undertone to John Moss.

"Old man, she's got one scalp in de belt."

Twice more, before dawn broke across the skyline, that sinister howl of a coyote shattered the silence.

Then, as the new day filtered through the night's shadows, six stampeding horses, the stirrups of empty saddles flopping, tore across the mesa. Eagle Chief had set the besieging party afoot.

Six empty saddles. Six men, then, had been in the attacking party. Two of those men lay dead on the doorstep. If that coyote signal could be taken for true count, three others had died with the Sioux's knife between their shoulder blades. But one man remained.

Out near the corrals, a rifle barrel lifted with a white rag tied to its front sight around the end of the barrel.

"I quit!" called a hoarse voice. "I got aplenty!"

Even as the words drifted through the dawn, the man's voice broke in a rattling, scream. The quivering cry of a coyote, its notes thin with cruel victory, rose, filled the dawn, echoed into grisly silence. Another red scalp dangled at the beaded belt of the Sioux warrior, its blood spotting the old Indian's naked thighs.

Eagle Chief, like some hunted animal, vanished from sight as the daylight came. He was miles away from the Ranch of the Four Winds by the time John Moss ventured outside to find him and somehow persuade the old Indian to cease killing.

"Old man, she'll come back tonight," prophesied Antoine.

Kathleen, white and frightened, yet meeting John Moss's eyes with a brave smile, prepared breakfast. Antoine helped John Moss carry the two dead men to the barn from the doorstep. They found the other four. Three of them had been stabbed. The fourth lay face downward in the stone corral, the feathered tip of an arrow in his back. All four had been scalped. The bodies were laid on a tarp in the barn.

"Antoine, we must stop this sort of thing. It's inhuman!"

Antoine shrugged and lit his pipe. "Old man, she's darn' hard *pour* to stop, *m'sieu*. She mak' de medicine. De star, she'll fall down 'bout de sky. *Pouf*, here you see den fellers dead. Old man's medicine, she's strong."

"But it's murder, Antoine."

"Me, I don't know 'bout what de white man call heem. De Injun, she'll fight lak' dat." Antoine scowled at the dead men under the tarp.

"Suppose, by gar, dem fellers she'll keel you and me. W'at den, eh, my good frien'? Dem fellers purty mean. W'at you theenk become of White Fawn, eh? Not so good, eh? No. Planty bad *pour* dat baby girl. White man, she'll say ees all right *pour* you and me to shoot dem fellers weeth de gon. *Out*. Dam' brave to stay in de house, poke de gon trough de hole, shoot de man outside. *Oui*. De bullet, she can' come into de house. No, no, no. House, she's made from the rock. Me and you stay in de house. Smok' de pipe, heat de grob and de black coffee. Strong mans. *Oui*." Antoine

250

pointed outside with an impressive gesture. "Injun, she go alone. No rock house to keep off de bullet, no gon, no grob *pour* de empty belly, no smok' *pour* de pipe, no black coffee weeth de planty sugar. No, by gar. Jus' one old man weeth de knife and de arrow. Tak' de dam' beeg chance. One man agains' planty bad fellers weeth gons. *Oui*, by gar. Old man mak' de crawl on de empty belly lak' snake. Jomp de white man who have planty gon. Mak' de fight. When he keel dat man, lift de hair. She's strong heart, dat old man. *Oui*. But de white man in de rock house, planty safe, she'll call dat old man, de Injun who have de bad heart. Sometam', *m'sieu*, me, Antoine, I'm not onderstan' 'bout dat."

Turning, the big old half-breed walked to the house. John Moss followed, scowling thoughtfully, the white man's mind trying to follow the red man's reasoning. Was not Antoine more than a little right? Had not that old Indian, well past the prime of life, pitted his wits and fighting craft against big odds? A man's life taken, be it by bullet from the front or a knife in the back, is killing. The grisly habit of scalping one's kill, according to the lights of the Indian, is but the tally of his skill and cunning as a warrior. In the white man's hospitals bodies are dissected in the name of medical science. White men's hangings in the name of the law are but a life for a life. What odds, the manner of that life's forfeit? In the eyes of Him who said — "Thou shalt not kill." — who was not guilty?

CHAPTER
THIRTEEN

Kathleen O'Day had seen the two men carry those dead men into the barn. The horror of death was written in her eyes as John Moss held her quivering body in his arms. And this was the house of peace, the house of council where men hung their guns on wooden pegs as they entered, then sat as men were meant to sit, words of truce on their lips.

Horror and fear finally found relief in terrible sobbing as John Moss held her close, his face hard and stern, yet softened with pity.

"It's all over, dear, all over. I promise you. I'll find a way, somehow, to end this killing. You've been brave and wonderful. You've stood it better than I hoped. But it's over."

Antoine looked puzzled. A faint smile spread his wide mouth as he heard John Moss promise the impossible in all sincerity.

From outside came the nicker of Scarlet, coming for his morning's feed of barley. Two other horses followed the big bay. Eagle Chief's horse was nowhere in sight.

"Old man tak' long ride, mebby." The half-breed nodded.

"Antoine," said John Moss, "I'm going for a short ride myself. You stay here. Don't admit any one except a friend."

"Where are you going, John?" Kathleen O'Day wondered.

"I'm going to stop this killing, if it's humanly possible. Don't worry, I won't get hurt."

John Moss had come to a decision. To Antoine that decision was nothing short of suicide. Kathleen, however, had faith in the man she loved.

She kissed him good bye bravely, faith and hope in her eyes. Antoine gasped when John Moss handed over his guns.

"What I am about to do, Antoine, cannot be done with a gun."

He rode away, smiling, straight-backed, unarmed. Even Antoine was moved to admiration.

"She's strong man, dat John Moss . . . de stronges' dam' man I'm evair know."

The man on the bright bay horse was lost in the blaze of the sunrise. Unarmed, with peace in his heart, it was as if John Moss rode forth on some crusade. It was a picture that would remain always in heart of the girl who waved him farewell.

Because his trail led straight to Mormon Creek, he did not pass a certain knoll where stood a naked Indian. Eagle Chief, Assiniboine-Sioux, lifted his arms to the rising sun. His lips chanted a death song. Erect, blood streaming across his bare chest from a bullet wound, he gazed with glazing eyes at his final sunrise.

253

The song died away. The naked body slowly sank among the rocks. Eagle Chief, the warrior, was dead. His spirit rode the shadow hills. His pony grazed a while, then trotted away. The medicine dream of Eagle Chief had come true.

Across the hills, at the adobe ruins on Mormon Creek, two men stepped from behind their shelter. The sunlight caught and reflected the steel of two gun barrels. So they stood, Barlow Burkett, the old he-wolf, and Sim Waldron, the last of his feudist clan. No words broke the silence. The guns tilted upward, spitting red flames. The men sank slowly, shooting as they fell, shooting as they lay there on the ground, until their guns were empty.

They had died according to their code, after the manner of their breed. The Waldron-Burkett feud was done.

Silence, unbroken save for the chatter of birds and the distant bawl of a cow, met John Moss as he rode slowly down the ridge to the adobe walls on Mormon Creek. The lone rider from the Ranch of the Four Winds, a white flag of truce fluttering from a lancelike shaft, had come too late. No living man remained to listen to his words. The Mormon Creek War had taken its toll of lives between two sunrises. The last of this range war was ended.

There was something of the prophetic about the coming of John Moss on this morning, unarmed, carrying the flag of truce, coming from the Ranch of the Four Winds where men sat in council. For in John

Moss, that new era that was to come found the man whose sincerity and strength became law. The Ranch of the Four Winds was to be the first courthouse in that district. John Moss was to become Judge Moss. Men of all manner of creed and color came to hang their guns on the wooden pegs, to sit before the fire and smoke. For when men are filled with excellent food and set fire to good Virginia tobacco, there can be more of peace than of hatred in their hearts.

John Moss stood with bared head above the dead body of Barlow Burkett. Some odd sentiment prompted him to take from his pocket that letter with its red seals. Slowly he broke the seals and read the contents:

To Whom it May Concern:

I hereby confess that it was me, Barlow Burkett, that done the four killings laid to Dion O'Day and Edward Moss. I was in Canada on the dodge for some killing in Texas. I took to trapping up in the Peace River country. Being raised among Injuns I got along good with them and lived amongst them.

I sold my catch to Dion O'Day and Edward Moss. They paid me fair. Then one day a Mountie rode up and began to arrest me for a fight I was in at Calgary. I up and shot him. I had to kill three more of them Red Coats before I dragged it for Arizona. I buried them all proper in the snow and went on my way. The Canadian government kept mum about those killings. But I got reason to know that they laid the killings to Moss and O'Day. That's partly why their free trading company went burst. That's why the Mounties was after them. Neither of them ever knew about those killings. It was me, Barlow Burkett, that done them.

When O'Day came here to Arizona, I took care of him. I likewise saw no harm came to the baby girl. Likewise, for a good many years it was me that kept the Waldrons from killing John Moss and burning down his place. They hated John Moss bad because they was ornery and he was square. By helping John Moss and O'Day and the girl, I aimed to square them Mountie killings that was laid to Edward Moss and Dion O'Day. Now I'm dead and they can't get me, so send this confession to Canada. It will take away that black bar off John Moss's pretty shield.

I have been a damn skunk but I reckon its in the Burkett blood. My daddy, was mean. Mebby this will kind of square things up. By the way I read the signs, John Moss is gonna marry O'Day's gal. That's good. I wish you both get fat and happy. I am hereby willing you, John Moss and wife, all my stock and land. No matter how I come by same, they can't take it away from you because most of them cows was stole from the Waldrons, and when I kick the bucket there won't be a damn Waldron left and you can bet on that.

I reckon this settles everything. Now that my missus and kids are gone all I ask is a chance to die shooting at a Waldron. So long, John Moss. You are a honest to God man.

I borreyed Edward Moss's ring from O'Day's young one to seal this. Just for a sort of test to see will John Moss keep his word, when he'll be faunching to read what's inside. I'm thinking he's man enough fer that and more.

So long,
Barlow Burkett

For several moments John Moss stood there, the scrawled confession in his hand, his face grave. He now knew why the Queen's government had placed the Bar Sinister across the shield of Moss. Sir Edward had never known. He had never understood. And those stern, proud, close-lipped British officials were loath to accuse openly such a man as Sir Edward Moss of murder. Nor would they disclose the knowledge of those four mysterious killings to the son of the man who stood accused secretly.

Just how much of their misfortune Edward Moss and Dion O'Day owed to the quick-triggered Barlow Burkett, no man could know. The old he-wolf had, in a measure, repaid his debt of sin.

Shorty's "Dyin' Day" was the blind Dion O'Day, and Burkett had sheltered him and found refuge at Montezuma Castle for Kathleen, Antoine, and Eagle Chief. He had saved the life and property of John Moss. He now willed his all to John and Kathleen.

And John Moss knew that it was not fear of prison or death that held Burkett silent through the years. He wanted to ride the hills until his gun had taken toll of the last of the Waldrons.

John Moss looked down at the dead man's face. Death had stamped a grisly smile of satisfaction on the mouth of the old he-wolf. He had died content.

Tomorrow men would come from Hackberry and gather the dead men for burial. They would call upon John Moss to preach the funeral sermon. They would gather at the Ranch of the Four Winds. There, while their guns hung from the wooden pegs, those bronzed, clear-eyed frontiersmen would smoke and talk, as some of them had talked before, of bringing law into that section.

Now, with the warring factions gone, their aims were possible. The hopes of men and the dreams of their womenfolk would assume shape. As John Moss was chosen to say the final few words above the bodies of those men who had died, so would he be chosen to judge the living.

John Moss rode slowly homeward in the bright sunlight of the glorious Arizona morning. His long quest was ended. The Bar Sinister no longer tainted the shield of the House of Moss. There at home waited the faithful Antoine who would again sing and laugh and sometimes go north to visit his friends along the Canadian line, to dance the Red River jig, and unfold strange tales of the great Southwest, to thump his great chest and say — "Me, Antoine, de stronges' damn' man in Quebec." — although he had never been to Quebec in his life. There, at the Ranch of the Four Winds,

Kathleen Mavourneen O'Day waited with love in her dark blue eyes.

So he rode homeward, his heart filled with happiness, his quest at an end — homeward, to that house where men shall sit in peace and blow the smoke from their pipes to the four winds.

About the Author

Walt Coburn was born in White Sulphur Springs, Montana Territory. He was once called "King of the Pulps" by Fred Gipson and promoted by Fiction House as "The Cowboy Author." He was the son of cattleman, Robert Coburn, then owner of the Circle C Ranch on Beaver Creek within sight of the Little Rockies. Coburn's family eventually moved to San Diego while still operating the Circle C. Robert Coburn used to commute between Montana and California by train, and he would take his youngest son with him. When Coburn got drunk one night, he had an argument with his father that led to his leaving the family. In the course of his wanderings he entered Mexico and for a brief period actually became an enlisted man in the so-called *gringo* battalion of Pancho Villa's army.

Following his enlistment in the U.S. Army during the Great War, Coburn began writing Western short stories. For a year and a half he wrote and wrote before selling his first story to Bob Davis, editor of *Argosy All-Story*. Coburn married and moved to Tucson because his wife suffered from a respiratory condition. In a little adobe hut behind the main house Coburn practiced his art and for almost four decades he wrote approximately 600,000 words a year. Coburn's early fiction from his Golden Age — 1924–1940 — is his best, including his novels, *Mavericks* (1929) and *Barb Wire* (1931), as well as many short novels published only in magazines that now are being collected for the first time. In his Western stories, as Charles M. Russell and Eugene Manlove Rhodes, two men Coburn had known and admired in life, he captured the cow country and recreated it just as it was already passing from sight. SQUARE GUNS will be his next Circle Ⓥ Western.

ISIS publish a wide range of books in large print, from fiction to biography. Any suggestions for books you would like to see in large print or audio are always welcome. Please send to the Editorial Department at:

ISIS Publishing Limited
7 Centremead
Osney Mead
Oxford OX2 0ES

A full list of titles is available free of charge from:

Ulverscroft Large Print Books Limited

(UK)
The Green
Bradgate Road, Anstey
Leicester LE7 7FU
Tel: (0116) 236 4325

(Australia)
P.O. Box 314
St Leonards
NSW 1590
Tel: (02) 9436 2622

(USA)
P.O. Box 1230
West Seneca
N.Y. 14224-1230
Tel: (716) 674 4270

(Canada)
P.O. Box 80038
Burlington
Ontario L7L 6B1
Tel: (905) 637 8734

(New Zealand)
P.O. Box 456
Feilding
Tel: (06) 323 6828

Details of **ISIS** complete and unabridged audio books are also available from these offices. Alternatively, contact your local library for details of their collection of **ISIS** large print and unabridged audio books.